Rico's Cat

Rico's Cat

by Dana Brookins

drawings by Mike Eagle

A CLARION BOOK

The Seabury Press / New York

The Seabury Press
815 Second Avenue, New York, New York 10017

Printed in the United States of America.

LIBRARY OF CONGRESS CATALOGING IN PUBLICATION DATA

Brookins, Dana.   Rico's cat.
"A Clarion book."
Summary: In St. Louis during World War II, a boy determines
to hide and raise his kitten, despite the landlord's firm rule
against pets on the premises.
[1. Cats—Fiction] I. Eagle, Michael. II. Title.
PZ7.B7898Ri   [Fic]   76-8841
ISBN 0-8164-3175-2

To Nuch.
And to the city of my birth,
St. Louis.

Rico's Cat

Chapter 1

I wasn't even thinking about the Mad Scientist the night we met the cat. And there weren't any signs then that that crazy cat would yank us deep into scary adventure.

Old Mr. Alpert, who took a walk every twilight and carried on loud arguments with himself, was strolling along the sidewalk. "That's right, Jake," he muttered. "You mark my word. We'll whip those Huns." It was the spring of 1943, and the American armed forces were a little over a year into World War II. But while Mr. Alpert's body walked a city street in the present, his mind charged through the battles of 1917.

My brother Rico and his girl friend Sally were playing a silly game of house on our front yard. We had no grass. Years of running feet had stamped down the poor blades until only hard dirt remained.

Sally had drawn the house with a stick, and she was now in the kitchen sweeping.

"You no good loafer," she shouted at her husband, my brother, who was nine. "All you do is drink beer, beer, beer." Whack went her broom on his bottom. I was twelve, and they seemed very childish.

Far up the block a whistle tooted. In a while, we would see a little red cart wheel up the street. An old man pushed the cart. He wore his white hair long, and a dashing mustache drooped to his chin. If I strained my ears, I could hear him shouting, "Tamales! Hot tamales!"

That was when the cat came right up the middle of the street, even though there were twenty shrieking boys darting around. She walked high on her toes with her pink nose pointed in the air.

"Cat!" Rico hollered. When that failed to break up the ballplayers, he shouted, "MAD DOG!" No words could be more frightening. We dreaded a mad dog almost as much as we feared rats.

Twenty boys ran for the safety of their yards. Smiling evilly, Rico left his stick-drawn house and raced for the street. "Cat, cat," he hollered.

The cat seemed to know he meant her. She stopped in the street, her tail pointing high and waving at the tip. The pink nose turned toward Rico. "She must be lost," I said sadly. I hurried to Rico's side and knelt in the street.

"Get away," he said fiercely. "This is *my* cat, Dee. I found her myself."

"You didn't *find* her," I snapped. "She's just right here in the street."

"Listen, I never had a cat in my whole life," he said flatly. "I'm going to keep this one." Strange things often came over Rico. He knew that Mr. Frisbie, the landlord in our four-apartment building, didn't permit pets. Mr. Frisbie couldn't even stand kids.

"Who wants to keep a fat cat, anyway?" Billy Loomis, my own private, wonderful boyfriend demanded.

"That's no mad dog!" Jimmy Grossinger snorted. "It's the fattest cat I've ever seen."

"She's going to have kittens," a voice said. My heart turned over. *Harold* stood among us. Harold was a young student at the Washington University Medical College near our home in St. Louis, Missouri. He lived up the street, and because medical students didn't have much money, my mother often invited him to dinner. I had fallen madly in love with him.

"I'll wait for you to grow up, and then I'll marry you, Dee," he had promised. "If you want me then instead of Billy Loomis."

"Billy's a child," I had sniffed, my eyes shining with love for this glorious doctor-to-be. I would be his nurse, and I would work long hours at his side, perhaps in the same faraway jungle.

"That cat's just fat," Jimmy Grossinger said. "I don't think she's even a girl."

"She's a girl," Harold said. He knelt down beside her and held out his hand. She looked at it for a moment. Then her round gray eyes met Harold's. "There goes her motor," Harold said. "She likes us."

"She likes *me,*" Rico said, clearly aggravated. "She's *my* cat." My brother wriggled his body until he squeezed between Harold and the cat. He reached out to touch her head, and she pulled her neck back into her shoulders.

"Hold your hand out, Rico," Harold commanded. "You can't choose a cat for a friend. She must choose you."

Rico didn't like anybody telling him anything. But he admired Harold. Once Harold had saved the life of a dog hit by a car. Rico drew back his hand and waited.

In a moment the cat stuck her nose into his palm, and in another moment she was rubbing her lop-sided body against his knees. "Is she really going to have kitties?" Rico's eyes shone. "Then I'll have a whole family."

"You're silly," I said a little jealously, because the cat had not chosen me. "Mr. Frisbie would never let you . . ."

"Mr. Frisbie's a Nazi," Rico said. That was the very worst thing he could think of at the moment.

"She'll have her family soon, I think," Harold said. "I'd say maybe four kittens."

"Four." Rico breathed ecstatically.

"They'll go to the pound," Jimmy announced with a fiendish smile.

Very slowly, Rico stood up. One foot shot out and cracked Jimmy a good one on the shin. It did my heart good to see Jimmy, who was the neighborhood bully, hop around screaming words that we often found chalked on the sidewalk. "That was a brave thing you did, Rico," I said.

"Shut up," Rico said gruffly. I held onto the urge to give my brother a short pop on the top of his head. Harold might think *I* was being childish.

"We'd better get her out of the street," Harold said. He lifted the cat gently and carried her up the steps that led to our front yard. A tumble of boys and girls followed him.

"Get out of my yard," Rico shouted. "You're bothering my cat!" Nobody paid any attention. No one ever paid any attention to Rico. Only me. I had to live with him. I even had to sleep in the same room with him.

Harold gave the cat to Rico, and we went into the building. At least twenty of our friends tried to do the same, eager to see what would happen. I knew what would happen. When Mr. Frisbie saw the cat, he'd go berserk.

In my heart I wished we could keep the cat. She was pretty, with an orange circle around one eye and a black one around the other. "A calico," Harold called her. But I knew how foolish Rico was to get his hopes up. Mr. Frisbie looked like a mean grizzly bear with shaggy eyebrows and eyes that never smiled beneath them, and he had a voice like ten river foghorns.

"What in the world!" my mother cried when she opened the door of our apartment. "Get that animal out of here. If Mr. Frisbie . . ."

But it was too late. "Mad Dog Frisbie," as Jimmy Grossinger always referred to him, had followed us up the steps, and we could hear his awful roar.

"Get home, brats!" Mr. Frisbie bellowed. Then, spying what was in Rico's arms he shouted even louder, "You give me that cat, Rico Haymacher!"

"Don't handle her like that," Harold commanded. But it was too late. Mr. Frisbie snatched the cat out of Rico's arms and marched back down the hallway.

"You dirty old Jap," Rico screamed over the railing. "You put that cat down! She's mine!" But Mr. Frisbie went right out the finger-smeared glass door.

Rico would have torn down the stairs after him, but my mother held him back. He fought with her a moment, his face full of anger, then suddenly he slumped against the railing. I was stunned to see tears in his black eyes. Rico never cried.

"I never had a cat before, Mama," he said.

"I know," she said. "I'm sorry, Rico." She looked helplessly at Harold.

"Come on, Rico," Harold said gently. "Come and show me your savings-stamp book."

Rico was proud of his stamps. He bought the stamps at the post office for twenty-five cents apiece because the money helped our government win the war. But now he only gave Harold a terrible look. "She *chose* me," he said fiercely, and went inside the apartment to stare out the front window at the yard below.

Mr. Frisbie carried the cat outside and then rounded a corner of the building, yelling that if anyone tried to follow him, there would be a thrashing. We knew he was turning the cat loose in the alley.

"She didn't even have a name," Rico said angrily. "I was going to call her Molly."

Chapter 2

There was a little time before dinner. Even though I felt sad about the cat, I would have gone back outside to play. But Harold had gone home to clean up before coming back to eat with us, so I decided I would polish my nails instead.

A half-hour later, all shiny-nailed, I realized I still had some time left. I listened to the shouts of the kids down below. If I went out, I knew I would chip my polish, and I wanted to be beautiful for Harold. A ribbon, I thought, and went to the bureau to hunt around on top. That darned Rico had let his stuff inch over the chalk line I had drawn to separate our sides. A broken airplane sat on top of my little pile of ribbons.

With an angry snort, I pushed it aside and picked out a blue ribbon. We had a small mirror hanging over the bureau. It was brown with age, but I could see that the ribbon made my eyes look twice as blue. I looked so good I decided that when I became Harold's nurse I would always wear a blue ribbon in my hair. I looked for something else to do, and my eyes landed on some papers sticking out from under my pillow.

"My book!" I cried. It was just the thing to work on while I was waiting for Harold.

I hurried over to the bed, annoyed with myself that I hadn't done a better job of hiding the book when I made up the bed that morning. I didn't want anyone to know I was writing it until I became world famous. Then I would give out autographs to everyone in the neighborhood.

I checked the living room. Rico was still sitting in the window, looking down on the street, his chin in his hands. I couldn't see his face, but I knew he was thinking about the cat. For a moment I felt sad again. Then something brilliant struck me. A cat! The perfect thing. In my book, Joe, a soldier, was going off to war, and he was looking for just the right present to give his girl friend Cynthia. I hurried back to my room, grabbed a pencil and started to write:

"Here is a cat for you, Cynthia," Joe said. "It is called a calico cat. I want you to keep it forever. If I do not come home from the war, you will have it to remember me by. Why don't you call it Joe?"

"Oh, Joe," Cynthia sobbed. "You must come back to me. But if you don't, I will always keep the cat to remember you by."

Having written those beautiful words, I cried a while for Joe. And especially for poor Cynthia who did not know what I knew, and that was that Joe was going to die in the war. He would be a hero and Cynthia would go right on loving him, even when she was an old lady.

I started reading my book again from the beginning while the smell of stuffed bell peppers filled the apartment. Down below an ice cream wagon tinkled by, and up the block someone cried, "Berries! First of the season!" The sun faded over the city.

At dinner, Rico was still upset over the cat, and Harold tried to keep his spirits up. My father was working late at his service station. In a little while he would come home and eat the peppers my mother had kept warm in the oven. Then the two of them would leave for the train station to pick up

Uncle Morris, who was coming into the city on business.

My mother watched as Rico poked at his food. Outside, it was dark, and I knew Rico's thoughts rested on the cat, out there somewhere, alone. I loved the city with my soul, but I would not have wanted to be alone in its alleys at night.

Rats roamed in those alleys—giant, beady-eyed creatures that slithered in shadows and dug in garbage cans. Some of the rats would be nearly as big as the cat herself. But what can you do when there are Mr. Frisbies in the world?

"Tell you what," Harold said, trying to cheer us up. "I believe I could spare some time from studying after dinner. We'll go downstairs, and I'll tell *The Tell-Tale Heart* again."

My own heart beat fast. Harold was the best story-teller in the world. Any other night Rico would have screamed with joy. More than anything, he loved to be scared. But tonight he went on staring at his still full plate.

After dinner we tromped outdoors. "Harold's here," I shouted to anyone within hearing distance. "Our Harold is going to tell *The Tell-Tale Heart*."

At the announcement, kids came running, shoving each other and scooting into the best listening spots on the porch. To my surprise, Rico gave up his place on Harold's left and sat on the edge of the crowd.

My father came home, a tall, tired-looking man. He stooped to touch Rico's shoulder and then to kiss me on the cheek and shake hands with Harold, and then went on upstairs. Harold started his story-telling with a few jokes. He kept that up until someone yelled in a fit of excitement, "Never mind that stuff, Harold! Get to the spook story." My parents came down on their way to Union Station, but I scarcely noticed them.

Then came *The Tell-Tale Heart.* Thump went that awful thing buried beneath a floor. Thump, thump! By the time that heart was pounding under the floorboards, two girls had already run home because they couldn't take it. I just scrooched proudly close to Harold, my intended husband.

Too soon the magical half-hour ended. Groans filled the air when Harold announced he had to study. "I'll read in your apartment, Dee," he told me. "I told your mother I'd stay till they got back from the station. Incidentally, you certainly look pretty tonight."

I straightened the ribbon in my hair. "I'll come up and sharpen your pencils for you."

Harold smiled. "Thanks," he said. "But you have an hour before you have to come up. I'll manage."

"Hey, Dee," kids cried. "What'll we do?"

I turned back to them, reluctant to let Harold go, but not wanting to miss this last hour outside before bedtime. Dark was the marvelous, mysterious time for city playing, when pale light drooped from lampposts and turned shadows into grotesque shapes, when sounds were muted, and lightning bugs winked in the yards.

Earlier I had not noticed the swirling fog-mist. But now, with my skin still crawling from Harold's story, I glanced uneasily up the street. Fog fingers inched up the lampposts. A few miles in the distance, the Mississippi River, that great, mud-colored creature, traveled its route to the sea. Once my father had driven us down to the river at night. The fog had been thick there, and the dark river seemed somehow alive. I was afraid of the river, and yet I loved it.

"Hide-and-seek!" someone shouted. I looked about warily. After Harold's story, I wasn't sure I wanted to hide alone in the night. But soon children were running from Jimmy Grossinger who was "It." Jimmy always cheated. He counted to a hundred by fives instead of ones.

"Come on," Billy Loomis hissed at me. He grabbed my hand and yanked me around to the side of our apartment building. We knelt in the shadows there, holding hands, and in my bliss I forgot the fog and my fear and even Harold. Fickle person that I was, when I was with Billy Loomis, I loved him desperately.

Out on the street a car screeched as someone ran for "home." Mrs. Hall, who lived down the hall from us and worked the night shift at the bakery across the street, came out of the building. "You maniac!" she shouted at the driver. With yards barely the size of a small rug, we city kids had to do most of our playing in the streets, and every day the newspapers mentioned that some child had been run down.

One by one parents began to call their children home. "Tomorrow night we'll play post office," Billy promised grandly. I went upstairs sighing with love, and then I saw Harold bending over his books, and my heart began to beat for him again.

"Where's Rico?" he asked absently.

"Isn't he up here?" I said. I tried to pull a picture of my brother playing hide-and-seek into my mind, but it wouldn't come. Rico hadn't played!

"Rico?" I called.

"He didn't come up," Harold said. He went to the window, and I followed. We stared down into the quiet street. Only fog moved down there now. "Rico!" Harold hollered out.

"He must be at Louie's," I said quickly. Louie Loomis, Billy's little brother, was Rico's best friend.

Harold hurried to the phone and asked the operator for the Loomis apartment. Moments later he hung up. "Go see if he's at Sally's," he commanded. I ran across the hall to Sally and Marilyn Hall's door.

"I saw you holding hands with Billy," Marilyn, who loved Billy too, said icily. "And I'm not talking to you. Rico isn't here," she added.

"Can I help it if Billy loves me?" I shouted angrily, when she slammed the door in my face. "He isn't there," I told Harold.

"Who else can we call?" Harold asked, and for

the next ten minutes we telephoned our neighbors. No one had seen Rico except Jimmy Grossinger, who said Rico had disappeared during *The Tell-Tale Heart*.

Then came a timid knock at the door. Sally Hall stood there, her blue eyes round and scared. "I'm not supposed to tell you this," she said. "Rico said he'd kill me if I did. He said he was going to run away and find the cat, and then he was going to live with her on a farm because he hates the city. He said he hates the city because it's got Mr. Frisbie in it."

"Oh, Lord," Harold mumbled. I stared at him in fascination. Harold never swore. "Then he's probably roaming the alley looking for her."

"Roaming the alley?" I gasped. "Rico?" Then I remembered that Mr. Frisbie had turned the cat loose in the alley. I thought of the alley at night and of Rico out there someplace alone, and a shuddering thrill ran through me.

Chapter 3

"Come on, Dee," Harold exclaimed. "Get your Dad's flashlight. We've got to find him before your folks come back."

"Do you think Rico's really run away?" I asked, as I followed him into the hallway.

"He was pretty angry with Mr. Frisbie today," Harold said over his shoulder. "And he was awfully concerned over the cat being out alone, what with her babies due soon. But it's my guess he'll have trouble finding her. She got a pretty good start on him."

Billy Loomis was still on my front stoop. Alone. Maybe he was sitting down there pining for love of me. But I didn't have time to think about that now. "Hey, Billy," Harold called. "Come help us look for Rico."

"Rico?" Billy demanded.

"He's missing," I said importantly. "I think we're
—uh—going into the alley." For the first time, that
realization struck me. The alley! The only time I
went near the alley at night was when I had to
empty garbage out by the ashpit. None of the other
kids liked it either. Nobody ever had to search the
alley when we played hide-and-seek because nobody
would go near it. Who wanted a rat running up
their leg?

"*You're* going into the alley?" Billy exclaimed.

"Well, it's my brother who's missing," I said
bravely, trying not to notice the fog. Usually, I had
practically no feelings for Rico. Hadn't he just this
week stolen the perfume out of my best hobnail
bottle and replaced it with water and sold the perfume to a girl in the fourth grade for a quarter? And
hadn't he bought himself five Milky Way bars with
the quarter and gobbled them all before I found out?
Still, I was learning how it is with brothers and
sisters. Tomorrow night I might hate Rico again,
but I wanted him safe and sound where I could hate
him. "I'm going," I insisted.

"Let me get my flashlight," Billy said.

"Hurry up," Harold said impatiently. Billy was

20

back a couple of minutes later, not only with a flash-light but with his father too.

"Can I help?" Mr. Loomis asked.

Upstairs, a window went up. "What's going on?" Marilyn called suspiciously. "Is that you, Billy and Dee?"

"Rico's missing," Billy hollered back. "We're going looking for him."

"Keep it down," Harold said gently. "No point in alerting the whole neighborhood. We may find him right off."

We walked toward the back yard, and I kept trying to make out familiar things in the grayness. But it was like being cast adrift with nothing to anchor yourself to. Once I bumped into the side of the house; it felt damp and slimy, and I had to choke back an "Oh!"

We moved in a little clump through the side gate. "Dee," Harold said. "Mr. Loomis and I will hit the alley. You and Billy look in your basement. It might have occurred to Rico that the cat could get down there."

"The—uh—basement?" I muttered.

The basement was always huge and black and

scary, especially at night. Who knew for sure that the Frankenstein monster wasn't real? Who could not say that some night he might get loose and hide down there?

"Gee, wouldn't Rico be long gone from there?" Billy demanded. He wasn't any fonder of basements than I was. But Harold and Mr. Loomis had moved off into the gray.

"Well . . . ," I said.

Just then we heard the side gate, and Marilyn came flying out of the fog. "I'll go into the basement with you, Billy," she said sweetly. *"I'm* not a sissy, and it isn't even my brother that's lost."

"Did I say I wasn't going?" I snapped. I shoved open the screen door and groped to the head of the black stairs. I found the light switch on the wall, but it didn't help much; it only threw pale shadows against the gloom below. For just an instant all three of us wavered, and then I plunged ahead of them again, rushing down the stairs to the cement floor. Forgetting that we were enemies in love with the same boy, Marilyn caught up with me and grabbed my hand.

In the basement there were four monstrous furnaces, one for each apartment. In the winter the men in the building were up before dawn, shoveling coal into the gaping iron mouths. Now, in the spring, the furnaces stood cold and silent.

Behind each furnace was a bin for coal. At the back of the basement were four small rooms called lockers, built out of wooden slats. Since we had no garages, this was where people stored the things they did not want to keep upstairs.

Billy flipped on the flashlight he had gotten by sending in box tops off cornflakes. It made a weak, spindly light that darted between the slats.

"Help!" Marilyn screamed suddenly. Billy had moved a couple of steps ahead of us, and he fell over his own feet scrambling back into line. "What is it?" he shouted at Marilyn.

"There's a body in that locker!" she moaned.

I was on the verge of bolting, but I didn't. "Flash the light again," I commanded. Then I snorted with a lot more courage than I felt. "It's only that old dressmaker dummy," I cried. "Good night, Marilyn! You know Mrs. Alpert keeps her junk down here."

Billy didn't make a move to start for the lockers

again. "Rico isn't here," he announced. "We would've seen him." Thrilled with relief, we all tore for the steps. All three of us jumbled there a second before Marilyn clawed her way to the front and came outside first. I took in a huge breath of the night air and felt a tiny tweaking of pride. Maybe I didn't like the basement at night, but I'd gone down.

Something amazing had happened in our backyard in the short time we had been gone. A dozen men were milling around, their flashlights making circles of light in the fog.

Mr. Loomis was back in the yard. "I'm not sure Harold thinks we need to make a major thing out of this," Mr. Loomis said. "But a couple of people saw us out their back windows and came out to see what was up, and one thing is leading to the other, the way it often does."

"Rico's missing!" The cry went up the block.

Old Mrs. Alpert, who lived in the past with her husband, leaned over her downstairs windowsill and shouted in a quaky voice, "What's happening? Is the war over?"

Harold appeared in the patch of light Mrs. Alpert's raised shade allowed. "All right," he sighed.

"Maybe we are going to need help. It's a pretty nasty looking night." He took over the organization of the searchers.

My relief over getting out of the basement didn't last long. "Some of you men take the other basements," Harold commanded. "The rest of us will finish covering the alley."

"The alley?" I mumbled.

"My mother's calling me," Marilyn insisted, and ran back for the front of the building, evidently no longer caring if I had Billy all to myself.

"Come on, kids, if you're coming," Mr. Loomis said to Billy and me.

Billy and I squared our shoulders and walked toward his father, like soldiers going to battle. Like Joe in my book, I thought, walking straight and tall. Then I remembered that Joe was going to die, and I sneaked an uneasy look toward the long stretch of alley that was nothing but fog and a few bobbing lights.

I had never been permitted in the alley at night, as if I would have gone even *with* permission! The beam from Mr. Loomis's light probed ashpits as we walked, coating them in eerie yellow. Here and there a rat, bold and stuffed from its foraging, sat on the edge of one of those brick constructions that held our trash. Beady eyes gleamed at us.

"You know where Rico might be?" Billy whispered suddenly at my side.

"Where?"

"The Mad Scientist's got him."

Chapter 4

"Oh, no!" I groaned. I stopped in my tracks. Far up the alley I could sense if not see the place where the Mad Scientist lived. It was an ancient building made of faded bricks, with two single windows on the upper floor that always seemed like watching eyes. Even in daylight kids would not walk beyond the fence to that awful place.

It had been part of a barn before Civil War days, a place, rumor had it, where runaway slaves had been hidden, only to be betrayed and sold back to their owners. It was a fitting place for HIM.

No one had ever seen the Mad Scientist up close, of course. But for blocks around any kid could tell you that if you wandered too near the old barn you were lost. At one time or another we'd all run through the alley, only to be brought up short by the sight of his evil face peering around the corner of one cracked window.

No one knew exactly what the Mad Scientist did behind those brick walls. The house in front of his home faced the street behind us and had stood empty all the years I could remember. Some said it was haunted by the mournful ghosts of children the Mad Scientist had killed. And on Halloween, no child in his right mind trick-or-treated near that place.

The thought of Rico in the clutches of the Mad Scientist was horrifying. I came close to breaking into tears, but Harold, coming back, saved me from that shame. And from having to go on exploring.

"Dee," he said anxiously. "I'm afraid your folks will be back any time. You go on around front and wait for them, will you? Your mother's going to be upset, and she'll need you. The minute we find Rico, I'll send Billy running to tell you."

I fled back down the alley through our backyard gate, skirting the garbage can instinctively, and arrived at our front steps more grateful than I would admit. Old Mrs. Alpert was out front now. Wearing a dressing gown, she stood at the head of the steps, hand on the railing, her eyes staring straight ahead. "Let the Huns come," she cried in her thin voice. "We're ready."

"Poor soul," a woman mumbled. Mrs. Alpert had missed the point entirely.

Quite a crowd had gathered since we began searching. Kids too young or too scared to go into the alley grouped around our steps, reveling in the fact they were up way past bedtime. Most of them were in pajamas or robes. Rumors ran through the crowd as wildly as some that came about the war.

That very week we had heard that the Emperor of Japan, Hirohito, had committed hara-kiri. There had been great rejoicing on the block. The tamale man had given away free tamales. Men stopped on the street to shake hands with strangers, and kids sang in joyous frenzy, "We've licked the Japs. *Der Führer*"—which is what we called Hitler—"is next." But it had only been a rumor, and the very next day a radio announcer had told us in a tense voice how the Japanese had bombed the daylights out of one of our islands.

Now it happened with Rico. Someone came up the street with a boy in tow, and Sally yelled joyously, "They've found him!" But it was only Mrs. DeBasco coming to see what the trouble was and dragging her Marco along.

30

"I saw Rico's face at your window, Dee," a boy hollered. In a body, we raced up the stairs to our apartment, only to find it a false alarm.

Mr. Frisbie stuck his shaggy face out his door as we trooped back downstairs. "Get those people out of my front yard," he bellowed.

"They're just waiting for news," I said angrily. "Rico's lost."

"I know," he muttered. "Good riddance!" He banged his door shut.

Downstairs, Mrs. DeBasco had taken it on herself to explain the true situation. "Rico?" Mrs. Alpert demanded. "Rico who?"

In a few minutes, Harold came around front looking worried. "We've searched the whole alley, Dee." Then, after a short hesitation, he said, "I'm going to have to call the police."

"Police!" rippled through the crowd.

Harold went upstairs to make the call. Marilyn ran across the street to the bakery to tell her mother about Rico. Mrs. Hall came back with her, carrying a tray of warm bread fresh from the ovens for everybody. Mrs. DeBasco ran home to bring the coffee she'd just made. By the time the police arrived, she was already offering it to the men returning from the alley.

Boys and girls swarmed around the squad car. Two burly officers got out, and Harold rushed to huddle with them.

"What uniform is that?" Mrs. Alpert demanded. "Are those men spies? Rico *who* is lost?"

Now the men fanned out across the street. The whole block blazed with lights, and the smell of coffee filled the air. The fog grew colder, so that we all shivered. But the crowd doggedly kept up its vigil.

Then a terrible thing happened. In the excitement of the police arrival, I had entirely forgotten my parents. Now my father's old Pierce-Arrow, elephant of all cars, chugged up to the curb. "Please, don't scare my mother," I said to anyone in hearing range.

My parents and Uncle Morris got out of the car and stared in bewilderment at everyone. The crowd fell back solemnly to let them pass. "Don't panic, dearie," Mrs. Alpert shrilled. "But your brave son, Rico, is missing in action."

"Rico's lost!" someone cried.

"Dee?" my mother exclaimed.

I stepped to her side. "It's going to be all right, Mama," I said swiftly. "He was upset about the cat. But everyone's looking. They'll find him." She put an arm around me and pulled me close.

Uncle Morris had gotten out of the car with a jolly smile on his face. But now the smile faded, and he said, "Come upstairs, Ada."

"No," my mother said. "I want to be here when he comes up the street." She sat down on the stoop, and I sat down beside her as my father went off to help with the search.

"We're going to need something to rejoice with when Rico's found," Uncle Morris said, and he went up the street to an all-night grocery store and came back bearing sacks of beer and wine.

"Go and sit with your friends," Uncle Morris said kindly to me. "Let me talk to my sister and remind her of an ancient time when I pulled something exactly like this." He nudged me out of my place and patted Mama's hand.

As the long minutes crept by, I thought of the Mad Scientist again. I wondered if he *had* gotten Rico? I was sitting on the ground, forlornly watching Mrs. DeBasco eat a slice of bread, when a voice suddenly demanded, "What's going on?"

"Rico's lost," somebody said automatically.

"I'm not!" the voice said angrily. "I'm right here."

"Rico!" someone cried happily.

I stared in dumb surprise at my brother and leaped to my feet. He stood in the center of the crowd, his hands thrust deep into his pockets.

With a wild, glad cry, I threw myself at him. "Oh, Rico! Nobody knew where you were."

"*I* knew where I was," he said. "I *always* know where I am. Stop hugging me."

Anger hit me. "You were lost," I shouted at him. "You ran away."

"I didn't either run away," he said hotly.

"Sally said . . ."

"Sally's a big fat liar." Sally stared at him with wide, surprised eyes. "I was sleeping in the basement. I went down to get me some old comic books from the locker and I fell asleep."

"In the night?" I said, not believing a word. "Richard Haymacher, you're lying. You went looking for the cat."

"Phooey on that dumb old cat," he said.

He stamped his foot. "I wasn't lost," he insisted.

"We looked in the basement," I shouted into his face. I wanted nothing more now than to shake his teeth loose for scaring me.

"Ha, ha!" he shouted right back at me. "You came down and Marilyn started screaming for help, and you and those big sissies nearly killed each other trying to get up the steps. I'll bet you thought there was a monster down there. Well, there wasn't."

"Oh, you terrible little brat," I hissed. "You *were* there. But you weren't asleep."

"I was too. I heard you in my sleep."

My mother settled the argument. She grabbed Rico into her arms and hugged him fiercely. A second later she was pounding the stuffing out of his knickered bottom. "Don't you *ever* scare me like that again!" she hollered.

People started returning from the search. "Come on upstairs," Uncle Morris called. "Libations on me!"

Chapter 5

In the morning the whole neighborhood still buzzed with the excitement of the night before. My father and Uncle Morris and Mr. Loomis and some of the other men had sat up late drinking beer and wine. Uncle Morris had sung "The Marine Hymn," and Mr. Frisbie pounded on our floor, which was his ceiling, with a broom handle in a feeble attempt to silence the merrymakers.

By the time I left for school, my whole body felt like Dracula had drained the blood out of it. My eyes kept drooping shut at the breakfast table. I even thought I saw Rico slip his bacon into his pocket, but I was too tired to really notice.

Marilyn and I dragged ourselves off to school together. The noise had kept her up too, and she had dark circles under her eyes. We walked hand-in-hand, because in the mornings we always liked each other. Billy Loomis went to a Catholic school, not to our public school, so we didn't compete for him by day.

Jimmy Grossinger met us with a disgusted look on his homely face. "My father says there ain't any Mad Scientist. Him and Mr. Loomis went into his lab last night, and they went in the haunted house, too."

"Your father's crazy," Marilyn said.

Jimmy stuck his nose up close to hers. "You take that back!" he hollered. "If you weren't a stupid girl, I'd sock you."

"You couldn't punch your way out of a paper bag," Marilyn retorted.

"If you're so sure"—I baited him—"why don't we all go around to the alley and wait for *you* to go inside and see for yourself?"

Jimmy looked scared, and he tried to cover it up with a quick laugh. "I'll take my dad's word," he said. "He says there's only some old mats and a few hunks of stale bread and junk in there. He says some old bum must be using the lab—that place—to sleep." Nevertheless, we caught the way Jimmy's eyes moved uneasily in the direction of the alley. Personally, I didn't believe his father had gone into the Mad Scientist's laboratory at all.

Just as we reached the schoolyard at the end of the block, a truck pulled up and three men began to unload a strange contraption. The men hauled out a big mass of chain and a scoop made out of iron and set them up on the schoolyard.

"It's the scales!" Marilyn squealed.

"Scrap Day, Scrap Day!" kids hollered. Today our school would get behind our allies in earnest. It was our turn to go out into the neighborhoods to gather scrap metal for the war effort. People were eager to donate the junk in their cellars. Who knew when an old lamp might be melted down and wind up as part of a B-29 bomber? Old ladies who had no sons to send to war often would haul out old, heavy tables with metal legs. Burned-out irons, toasters, and even sandwich grills went to war.

Teachers were already on the playground discussing organization. Our principal, Mr. Bodgewell, a silver-haired man, was directing the placing of the scales with a voice like a general of the army.

At ten o'clock the whole school gathered on the playground, bunched into classes. We all carried empty paper bags. Some of the boys had wagons to pull, and a truck, manned by two of the fathers, stood ready in case someone, in a fit of glorious patriotism, should want to donate something as huge and dramatic as an old iron stove. Miss Sheehan, my teacher, announced that she had drawn maps of the city blocks to be covered. "We must get this war over in a hurry," I heard her say.

At ten-fifteen, a whistle blew, and everybody lined up. Miss Sheehan handed out our maps.

"Grades Seven B and Eight B, cover Elmwood Place," Mr. Bodgewell ordered, and off my room went. Someone began to sing the Air Force hymn, "Off we go, into the wild blue yonder. . . ."

The moment we hit Elmwood Place, my classmates scattered like busy ants. We ran from house to house, solemnly announcing at each door, "We are the seventh grade, and we are doing our bit for the war effort."

From cellars came hoarded treasures, picture frames made of metal, old pieces of jewelry. Jimmy Grossinger turned bright purple when an old lady presented him with a corset that had metal stays. What a glorious morning!

Our hearts swelled every time we realized we were actually helping those brave boys fighting in the Pacific jungles and in North Africa. "There's a private bomb for Hitler!" someone would yell, throwing a fireplace screen into the truck.

By noon we were exhausted but happy, and on our way back to school. We still marched proudly, if a little limply. Our faces were grimy, our backs ached from too much lifting, but our wagons were piled high, our sacks were bulging, and there were no less than two great black stoves on the back of the truck. No army had ever come back from a more glorious battle.

On the schoolgrounds everyone sat in little groups, munching sandwiches, watching the men weigh the scrap. "The best haul this week," one of them hollered. Who cared about aching bones?

The rest of the afternoon was a letdown. The excitement of the night before, added to the glory of the morning, caught up with me. All through Arithmetic, I dozed in my seat, lulled by the distant sound of metal still being weighed.

Miss Sheehan jarred me out of a beautiful dream in which I was the first woman pilot in the war. Harold was my copilot and Billy my bombardier. We were singlehandedly about to win the war when Miss Sheehan shook my shoulder.

41

"Dee, you're going to have to go home and get Rico," she said.

"Rico?" I mumbled.

"He didn't come back from afternoon recess," she explained. "Miss Limkin just sent a messenger to ask if you'd go get him."

"Not again," I moaned. Rico only stayed in school as long as things went his way. If he didn't like a lesson, or if Miss Limkin refused to read a story on a particular day when she had promised, or if she tried to tell him he didn't give the proper answer to a question when he knew he was right, he simply left class and went home. At least twice a month Miss Limkin sent me after him. There wasn't any use in calling our apartment because my mother worked afternoons at a laundry on the other side of the city.

I reluctantly headed homeward. A sparrow, fat from good March digging for seeds and bugs, chirruped from his perch on the telephone wire. But I was too tired to notice the beauty of city spring. Climbing the front steps, I thought fondly of my bed.

Rico met me at the glass door. He started at the

sight of me and quickly wiped his hands on his shirt. Ten streaks of dirt remained. "You little brat!" I hollered. "You're going to make me miss the sixth chapter of *Great Expectations*."

"I'm not a baby," he ranted at me. "I can find my way back to school."

"What'd you come home for in the first place?" I demanded.

"None of your beeswax, you creep!" he snapped. Pushing past me, he headed back toward the school.

I chased after him yelling, "I'm going to tell Mama!"

Rico whirled and planted his hands on his hips. "If you do, I'll tell her you kiss Billy Loomis in the gangway."

"You brat!" I sputtered.

"Sticks and stones," he sang, resuming his walk, "may break my bones, but words will never hurt me."

"Maybe words won't, but this will," I shouted, and flung a rock at him. It missed, and his laugh came back to me.

I didn't tell on Rico that evening. I hardly ever complained to Mama (Rico called it tattling). If I spent my time telling her things Rico was doing that he shouldn't, it would take up half my life. Besides, my mother was looking what she called "draggy." Her eyes had dark shadows, and she seemed uninterested in things. When I was helping her with dinner, she kept pausing in front of the stove to stare at the lightbulb hanging from the ceiling. I had to remind her to stir the pot.

Uncle Morris came into the kitchen while we were cooking. He was a big man with a big face, and his nose had turned bright red during the night and stayed that way all day. He had finished his insurance business in the city and would be heading back home early in the morning. For a little while he sat at the kitchen table, trying to keep his cigar ashes from flicking onto the oilcloth, asking me riddles. Rico heard and came in from the bedroom where he was supposed to be cleaning out his underwear drawer.

"What's black and white and red all over?" Uncle Morris asked.

"The Nazi flag!" Rico bellowed.

"No, no, no!" Uncle Morris chuckled. "You've got the war on your brain. It's a newspaper, Rico. Get it? Read all over. R-e-a-d!"

"Phooey," Rico said. "I knew that joke when I was born."

"Rico, don't sass Uncle Morris," Mama said absentmindedly. While the jokes went on, from time to time she would stop and give Rico a look that for some reason made me feel sad.

Uncle Morris saw it, too, and grew thoughtful, and in a little while he took Rico and me into the living room to wait for my father.

"Rico, I don't want to make you feel guilty," Uncle Morris said. "But I hope you won't ever worry your mother again the way you did last night. It's a pretty hard thing to believe your boy is lost somewhere in a big city. One time when your cousin Charles was four, he got away from me at a zoo, and don't think I didn't have some bad moments wondering if he'd been kidnapped or run over or some awful thing."

"I didn't mean to scare Mama," Rico said.

Uncle Morris ruffled his dark hair. "I know you didn't, son. To you it was probably like an adventure, right? Like old Huck and Tom off on the Mississippi?"

Rico nodded eagerly. Then Uncle Morris pulled two big silver dollars out of his pocket. "Well, you can have plenty of adventure without fretting your mother," he said. Then he handed each of us a dollar.

After dinner was over, I could hardly drag off to bed, I was so tired. But in bed I lay awake a few minutes, thinking about what Uncle Morris had said. And just before I fell off asleep, I made a big decision. In my book, Joe's mother had been going to get the telegram saying Joe had been killed. Now I changed my mind. "I'll make him an orphan," I mumbled.

"Who?" Rico said from his bed against the other wall. Sleep saved me from having to answer.

Chapter 6

Strange things began to happen after that day. First, the bedspread I had embroidered two years ago for my doll buggy disappeared. I didn't play with dolls anymore except when no one was looking. But I kept the buggy in a corner of our room for old times' sake.

"Who would steal your doll spread?" my mother demanded.

"Rico would," I said. "He probably sold it." But all my questioning and threats only brought a wicked smile to Rico's face.

When Mama started spring cleaning, she noticed that a cup and saucer made of bone china had vanished from high on a kitchen shelf. She spent that whole Saturday morning crying into her apron. "Your father's mother gave me that cup and saucer," she sniffed. "I always get it down when she visits. How will I explain?"

Other things drifted out of the apartment as though a ghost's hands were at work. A silk scarf with a big, buck deer in the middle and the word *Wyoming* on it disappeared from the living room. The pearl-handled brush Aunt Rachel had given me for Christmas vanished next.

But the final straw was a pair of horsehair gloves my father owned. He had gotten them for driving the first car he ever bought, and his rage over their disappearance was awesome. "There's a thief in this building," he ranted. Through it all, Rico only wore the same mysterious smile.

On Thursday, exactly a week after what the neighborhood referred to as "The Night We Lost Rico," Mr. Bodgewell announced that we would have a paper drive. Mr. Bodgewell had been carried away by the success of our scrap drive (we placed first in the city for pounds collected and Jimmy Grossinger claimed it was the stays in that corset that put us over the top). So he decided we should collect paper for the war effort, too.

Once again the school hummed with excitement.

Mr. Bodgewell did not believe in a moment wasted. The war could not wait for slowpokes. Our teacher wrote on the board, "Get behind our boys at the front. Tie your old papers up in bundles for our collection."

Overflowing with patriotism, I copied the message for my parents, embellishing the sides with little American flags. Marilyn made one for Mrs. Alpert. I made one for Mr. Frisbie. After all, I told myself, his paper must be as good as the next person's.

But when I showed it to Mr. Frisbie after school, he took one look at my message and fell into a fit. "Not *my* papers you don't," he fumed. "I keep them in my locker bin for making furnace fires in the winter." He shook an angry finger in my face. "Let 'em win the war without my newspapers. Haven't they got my old andirons your brat of a brother stole?"

If I had remembered the andirons, I wouldn't have been stupid enough to ask Mr. Frisbie for the papers. Three months ago, when Louie's Catholic school was collecting scrap, Rico, bursting with friendship and love of country, had taken it upon himself to raid all the locker bins in the basement. A pair of old motorcycle fenders my father was saving for his own reasons had disappeared. And Mr. Frisbie's andirons.

"You stole them, Rico," my father said. Which only caused Rico to retort, "It wasn't stealing. I *confiscated* them." There was no stopping Rico when patriotism came over him.

"Like you confiscated our tin cans," my father had said hopelessly. Everybody saved tin cans, flattening them out and storing them in big boxes. When the boxes were filled, we took them to collection points in various sections of the city. Once Rico had emptied over twenty cans of food from our cupboards into bowls and had personally stomped the tins into shape.

Mr. Frisbie's face turned positively purple as he ranted on about his andirons. Then suddenly a thought hit him. "My papers!" he gasped. "That brat is probably down in the basement stealing them right now." He grabbed my arm. "You come with me, missy." he bellowed. "I want a witness when I whale him."

I found myself yanked out the glass door, around

the building, and down the basement stairs. Just outside his locker bin, Mr. Frisbie hit the light switch.

"Rico can't be in there," I stammered. "You've got a lock on the door."

"Padlock didn't stop him before," he raved. "He took off a slat to get in!" In only a moment he had the lock opened and the door thrown wide. "Aha!" he shouted.

I blinked in the dim light. Then shock slammed through me. "Rico!" I gasped.

My brother sat on a pile of newspapers, his arms folded defiantly. "Get out of here," he said.

"Get out of here?" Mr. Frisbie roared. For a moment his anger was so great he couldn't even speak. He just stood there with his mouth working. Then he shouted, "Get out of my own locker?"

He reached for Rico and yanked him to his feet. "I'm going to teach you the lesson of your life!" he screamed. His hand was raised to whop Rico a good one, when suddenly a wild creature flung itself in front of him. I stared open-mouthed. It was the cat!

Her hair stood high on her back, and her upper lip curled above her teeth. She arched her body,

making sharp, hissing noises. One paw shot out, and she spat at Mr. Frisbie's foot. He jumped back, startled.

"Darn it, Molly," Rico shouted. "I told you to hide and protect your babies."

Mr. Frisbie found voice for one explosive word. "Babies?"

"You did this, Dee!" Rico stuck his face up near mine. "You told on me."

"I didn't either," I said hotly. "I didn't even know you were down here."

Mr. Frisbie had backed off from the fury-filled cat. But his eyes were sweeping around the locker. I watched him fearfully and saw them light on the edge of a cardboard box sticking out from behind a trunk. With a savage growl, he threw himself at the box and peered inside.

"What's this?" he gasped. "You've been in a box of things I keep down here." He yanked a strange thing out of the box. It was a pink baby sweater. "You *used* this?" he bellowed. "For *kittens* to sleep on?" Suddenly the cat bounded into the air, landing on one of Mr. Frisbie's legs as though it were a tree. She tried to sink her teeth through his pants.

"Get her off me," he bellowed.

Rico grabbed for the cat. "Bad girl, Molly," he hollered. "She's only trying to save her babies," he yelled at Mr. Frisbie, while he was trying to pry loose the determined mother.

A few moments of scuffle later, Rico had the cat in his arms and Mr. Frisbie was rubbing his leg. I had never seen his face darker. "I'll give you five minutes to get that animal and her kittens out of here," he said. "If I ever see her near this building again, I'll feed her to the river. *After* I kick you out of your apartment. And if you ever touch my things again, I'll feed *you* to the fish, Rico Haymacher." He backed off, the pink sweater clutched in his hand, his black eyebrows grown together in his terrible anger.

I had no time to puzzle over the sweater. "You better help me, tattletale," Rico commanded. "You carry Molly. I'll take her babies."

"I didn't tell," I insisted. But try and change Rico's mind once it was made up.

"Get them out to the alley," Mr. Frisbie thundered.

All of a sudden Rico's whole attitude changed.

He looked toward the two small basement windows that rose just above the yard.

"It's getting dark," he said. "Can't we keep her down here tonight, Mr. Frisbie?" I'd never heard him say Mr. Frisbie so respectfully. "Tomorrow I could find . . ."

"Out!" Mr. Frisbie roared. "Now!"

"We're going," Rico muttered. I caught a quick glimpse of his tongue darting out at Mr. Frisbie. Then he was gathering up the box from behind the trunk.

"I'm scared of this cat," I moaned. Rico had thrust her into my arms, and I could feel fear and anger running through her body.

"She won't bite you unless I tell her to," Rico said. He began to struggle toward the steps. Behind us, Mr. Frisbie did a strange thing. He sat right down on the floor and began to dig in the box of old clothes.

Chapter 7

Outside the back gate, Rico stood puffing and looking around. Suddenly I realized what he carried. "Kittens," I breathed. "Oh, Rico, let me see them. Oh," I moaned. "Rico, they're gorgeous."

There were four of them—two orange, one black, and a calico with a brown and orange butterfly on her face. Rico let me stroke each sleeping form before he snapped, "That's enough. I'm going to charge kids a penny apiece to pet them."

The mother began to struggle in my arms, planting her hind feet against my stomach and pushing hard. Rico set the box down, and she hopped inside and began to lick her children.

They came awake squealing, and she settled down beside them. The kittens tumbled over each other to get at her fluffy white underside.

"Let the runt in," Rico said in a chiding voice.

He knelt and pulled the tiny black kitten out from under the others. Then he held its nose to a pink nipple until it got the idea. A moment later it was sucking, its tiny paws digging at its mother's stomach. "That's Timothy," Rico said. "He's the only boy."

"*You* don't know if it's a boy," I said. "Hardly anyone can tell if new kittens are boys or girls."

"*I* can tell," Rico said imperiously. "Timothy's the only boy."

"I bet he has babies someday," I snorted. But Rico ignored me.

For a time we crouched there beside the box. Then suddenly I spied the corner of something bright. "Rico Haymacher!" I exploded. "That's my doll spread."

"So what?" he demanded.

"I want it back!"

His eyes narrowed. "You want me to tell Billy Loomis you still talk to that doll Brunhilda when you think I'm asleep?"

"You wouldn't!" I gasped. But his eyes flashed he would. Then I saw a piece of something black and hairy. "Daddy's horsehair gloves," I cried. "I'll bet you've got Mama's silk scarf, too. And my brush. And Grandma Mac's cup and saucer." Everything began to fall into place.

"They're all back in Mr. Frisbie's locker," Rico said. "I'll have to steal them out pretty soon. The brush is for cleaning Molly, and that ugly old deer is for covering up the babies at night, and the cup and saucer are for eating, and if you tell, I'll tell Billy how you bought that quarter valentine for yourself and signed it, "Your Secret Love" to make him jealous.

"I won't tell." I sighed. I got one of my urges to hold Rico up by his heels and pound him down hard on the head. But he had a nose for finding out secrets and I didn't want him to tell Billy about the valentine. "Rico, what are you going to do about the babies?"

"I don't know," he said. "It's getting pretty dark. I'm scared to leave them out here alone."

His eyes swept up and down the alley. Shadows had begun to creep out from buildings. Already rats were probably waking up in their underground caverns, hungry and ready for a night's digging in ashpits and garbage cans.

"I guess I could put them in the fort," Rico said.

Across the alley, on the edge of a back yard, Rico and Louie had dug a giant hole in the red dirt. On Saturdays they lay in the fort, powing away at pretend Japanese and Nazis with their wooden guns.

"I could put some boards over the fort," Rico said.

"What if it rains?" I demanded.

"It won't rain. It wouldn't dare," Rico said with a look at the skies. "You carry the kitties to the fort. I'm going down to the basement after Daddy's boards."

"That's wood he's saving for the furnace for winter," I said.

"So he can have it back. I'm just borrowing it."

I helped Rico fix up the fort house, holding boards while he nailed them together. In return he let me hold the calico kitten until he counted to a minute. "That's all the time you get free," he said. Then he slid the kitten box underneath the wood slats. "I don't like it," he said dismally. "If Molly can get out, a rat can get in after her babies."

He sat at the mouth of her fort home, staring into space. "I'll have to spend the night down here."

"You're crazy," I gasped. "Mama and Daddy won't let you. . . ."

"Who's going to tell them, big mouth?" he demanded. He gave me a black look. "I'll sneak down after we go to bed."

"I wouldn't stay in this alley after dark," I said, looking at the growing shadows. I'd had enough of alleys the night he was missing.

Behind the fierce look in Rico's eyes, I could tell he was scared. "I have to take care of my cat and her kitties," he said. And in spite of myself, I felt admiration for his loyalty. "Besides, I've been in the dark with her before," Rico went on. "The night her kitties got borned."

"That's where you were the night you disappeared!" I cried. "That's how you knew Billy and Marilyn and I were in the basement. Those kitties have been there over a week, and you never even told me."

"Why should I tell you?" he said hotly. "*I* borned them all by myself. Then he added, "Well, Molly and me together, I mean."

"How come they were in Mr. Frisbie's bin?"

"Try and tell a cat where to have her kitties. I found her in the alley that night, and I took her down to our bin, but she kept running off and getting into that box in Mr. Frisbie's."

"You were in the alley that night?" I breathed.

"She was crying for me," Rico said simply. "Listen, I'd do anything for a friend."

Our mother had come home from work, and her voice had joined the other voices calling in a you'd-better-come-or-else tone. Rico got up with one last fretful look at the fort home and started for our backyard. "I'm coming back out tonight," he said. "She'll be scared down here alone."

"You'll be spanked," I warned.

"Not unless somebody opens up her big trap."

We passed the ever-popular rat favorite, our garbage can, walking way around it, and went upstairs.

At dinner I watched Rico pocket part of his pork chop, and the truth dawned on me. No wonder Rico always looked greasy! And that day he'd come home from school, he must have brought part of his lunch home to the cat!

After dinner, Rico announced he was going to bed early. "Rico!" my mother exclaimed. She hurried to feel his forehead. "I'm just sleepy," he lied. Usually he had to be dragged to bed.

When I went into our room later, Rico was in bed. "Ha!" I cried. "You're scared after all."

When he didn't answer, I sneaked to my doll

buggy to kiss Brunhilda goodnight. I gasped. She was gone!

That was too much! Now Rico had stolen my doll. I flung myself at my brother to rattle his teeth out. Something hard met my hands. I flung back the cover, and there lay Brunhilda in Rico's bed. So he had already crept downstairs and left the doll covered up to fool anybody who looked into the room. Carefully, I replaced the cover and got back into my own bed, my mind on that dark alley and my brother down there alone. But I had no urge to go keep him company.

I don't know how long I slept before a piercing cry woke me up. It seemed to be coming from the alley. "Rico?" I heard my mother scream.

Chapter 8

Pandemonium broke loose in our apartment building. My father was out of bed in a flash and running in his pajamas for the back stairs. He carried the loaded pistol kept in a holster hung from the slats underneath his bed. He had bought the pistol when we lived in an old house that had bad locks on the doors.

Terrified, but bravely determined to help save my brother from whatever had got him (could the Mad Scientist have crept up the alley in the night and found Rico off guard?), I grabbed my bathrobe and ran for the back stairs. Marilyn and Sally clung together on the upstairs landing, sobbing wildly, "Don't let it get us, too!"

My mother was the first one into the back yard. Mr. Frisbie came right behind her, carrying a giant flashlight, the kind used by coal miners. "What is it?" he shouted. "Robbers?"

Up went Mrs. Alpert's window. "Are we being invaded?" she cried.

When I opened the back screen, something wild shot past my legs and into the basement. "Rat!" I shrieked and ran to grab hold of my father's pajamas.

"It's not a rat," Rico wailed. "That was Molly with a baby in her mouth. She's trying to save her kitties."

My mother grabbed for Rico's jacket as he tried to barrel through the back gate again.

"Let me go!" he hollered. "I've got to help them, Mama!"

"Help who what?" my mother cried. "Sam?" She stared pleadingly at my father, all the time Rico fought to free himself from her hands. "*Who* is Molly?"

Over his first shock and convinced there was no one to shoot, my father shoved his pistol into his big pajama pocket and knelt in the dirt beside Rico. He gripped Rico by the shoulders and shook him. "Snap out of it, son!" he ordered. "What's the matter with you? What are you doing down here this time of night?"

"Molly's the cat," I tried to put in.

"Cat!" Mr. Frisbie bellowed. "Is that cat trying to move into the basement again?"

Mr. Anastas, arriving home from his factory job, stopped off to see what the noise was. He lived four doors up the street. Already neighbors were gathering in our back yard. "It's Rico again," someone said. "That boy is a marvel for finding trouble."

"Let me go!" Rico went on shouting. "A rat got one of Molly's babies. I hit it with a stick and made it drop it, but I think it's dead."

Just then a fierce growl came from the back door. I turned in time to see Molly claw her way up the screen. With a grunt of rage, Mr. Frisbie threw himself at the door. When it opened, he snatched at the cat, but she sprang free and shot for the back alley, a calico streak in the beam of his giant light.

"She's going after the others," Rico hollered.

"Others!" my mother cried, blinking.

With a superhuman effort, Rico pulled himself free of my father's grasp and tore off toward the back alley. "He's going to the fort," I tried to explain to all the excited people. "That's where the other babies are."

"Babies?" Mr. Anastas demanded.

"What's going on?" Mrs. Alpert begged. "Do we have to take shelter?"

In that instant, Molly came racing back with something limp hanging from her mouth. She headed for the screen door, and Mr. Frisbie threw himself against it, his arms and legs spread out. "Oh, no you don't!" he shouted.

Rico was back, and he had the third kitten. "You let her go," he shouted at Mr. Frisbie. "That's our basement too. If you don't, a rat'll get her other babies."

"I own this building," Mr. Frisbie said, "and don't you forget it."

"Daddy!" Rico wailed.

My poor father, who had only barely heard of Molly and knew nothing about her babies, started shaking his head, and it kept on shaking as if he were a toy someone had wound up.

"Now let me get this straight," he said slowly. "This is a stray cat. . . ."

"She's not stray anymore," Rico said. "She's mine. Harold said she *chose* me."

"And this cat had kittens," my father went on, struggling with the puzzle he was trying to put together. "In the basement, I imagine, since she seems to want to carry them back there."

"I moved 'em out," Mr. Frisbie put in. "I hate cats."

"Mr. Frisbie moved them out," my father went on. "And now they're living in Rico's fort?"

"And Rico was afraid a rat would get them so he put Brunhilda in his bed so people would think it was him, and he came down here to spend the night to look after the kitties, but a rat must have got one anyway," I finished in a rush.

"I didn't know a rat got inside the fort," Rico said. "I don't see good in the dark. All of a sudden I heard Molly yell, and the next thing this rat came running out of the fort with one of the babies in its. . . ." His voice broke off. "The baby!" he gasped. "I figured it was dead when the rat dropped it in the alley, but maybe it's still alive."

Before anybody could grab him again, Rico raced out the back gate. My father followed him.

Mrs. DeBasco came up the street. "I heard the commotion," she said. Someone told her what was going on, and she tried to explain it to Mrs. Alpert in her window.

In a moment Rico and my father were back. My

father carried a piece of paper in his hands. A poor pitiful limp thing lay on top. Carefully, he laid it on the ground.

"He's dead," Rico said miserably. "It was the runt, Dee. Timothy. Molly's only son." In his hands Rico still carried the fourth kitten. It shivered and nuzzled his fingers. My mother knelt at the screen where Molly still tried to nudge past Mr. Frisbie's legs with a kitten in her mouth.

My mother held out her hands, and Molly raised her head, and gently let her kitten drop into them. "Oh, poor little things," my mother said softly. "They're freezing out here."

Molly hurried to Rico, sniffing the air. She seemed to know he held one of her children. Near the piece of paper that held the poor limp thing that had been Timothy, she paused. She lowered her head and for a long time the crowd stood quietly while she looked at her dead baby. Then she circled far around it and walked to Rico's legs.

"What's the matter with her?" Rico asked. "Doesn't she care if her baby's dead? She didn't hardly go near it!"

"She wants you to show her that the baby you're

holding is all right," my mother said gently.

"But doesn't she care. . . ?"

"Rico," my mother said. "She knows Timothy is dead. She knows there's nothing she can do for it. She's worried about her living children. Show her the kitten."

Rico knelt and held out the orange kitten. Molly sniffed it carefully all over and then lapped it with her pointed pink tongue. My mother came to kneel beside Rico. She held out the second kitten, and Molly licked that too. "Isn't there another?" my mother asked.

"In the basement!" Rico said suddenly. "She carried it down there."

"There's a cat in *my* basement?" Mr. Frisbie roared. He tore open the screen door and ran inside, and our father was right behind him.

"That man," Mr. Anastas said in his strong Greek accent, "he is a mean man. He hates too much." In her kitchen window, Mrs. Alpert had fallen asleep with her head resting on her chest. Mrs. Hall came home from the bakery across the street to check on Marilyn and Sally the way she did several times a night when they had to stay alone.

"What's Rico up to now?" she asked. Several people told her the story.

"I think we could use another cat at the bakery," she said, "if she's a good mouser."

Just then my father came outdoors carrying the kitten Molly had made it to the basement with. Mr. Frisbie was right behind him, his face so purple with anger he could barely speak. "She put it in my locker," he sputtered. "Right on top of my most important box of things. I wish a rat had got all of 'em."

For a moment I didn't see the terrible anger rising in Rico's face. But as my eyes got used to the dark, I could see the storm lines gathering around his eyes and mouth. Without a word he handed the kitten he held over to my mother. The crowd quieted again, aware that Rico was up to something new.

For a second he stood above the ragged little dead kitten. Then slowly he walked to where Mr. Frisbie was still fuming to anyone who would listen about how his basement had been invaded.

"It's all your fault," Rico said. "You wouldn't let Molly and her babies live in your basement. It's your fault Timothy's dead."

"Now just a minute, you whippersnapper," Mr. Frisbie sputtered.

"Rico," my father warned.

"Well, it's his fault, Dad!" Rico wailed. "They weren't hurting anything. They're just a bunch of kitty cats." I saw Rico's eyes narrow the way they did when he was really furious. Suddenly his arms shot up and waved at the apartment building.

"I put a curse on this house!" he shouted. I watched in admiration. Rico would have made a great actor. He'd gotten that line right out of a witch movie we'd seen last week.

"Wait a minute!" I gasped. "Rico, *we* live in this house too."

"Then I put a curse on Mr. Frisbie and Mr. Frisbie's apartment. Phht! Phht!" Rico jabbed his fingers toward Mr. Frisbie's kitchen window. Without another word he turned and began to gather up the kittens while Molly hovered at his feet, watching him with a worried look.

"Get a box," Mrs. Hall said. "I'll take them all over to the bakery and find them a nice corner. If the mother turns out to be a good mouser, she'll teach the babies to hunt too."

"They're *my* cats," Rico said. "Don't forget."

"I'm sure you can visit them all you like," she said kindly. "You're a good boy, Rico Haymacher. I never thought so before. But a boy who would spend the night in that dark alley looking after his cat friends can't be all bad."

In her window, Mrs. Alpert came awake. "Did we run 'em off?" she demanded.

"A curse," Mr. Anastas said slowly. "My, my, Mr. Frisbie. If I was you, I'd walk pretty careful from now on."

"Goodnight, everyone," my father said. "Rico's show is over for the night. Son, you find a box and go across the street with Mrs. Hall to settle the cats in their new home. I'll bury Timothy."

"Not in *my* yard," Mr. Frisbie shouted.

"In the alley then," my father said wearily. "In Rico's graveyard where he buried his snake and his goldfish last year."

"Come on to bed, Dee," my mother said. "It's been a long night."

On the way up the stairs I was careful not to walk too near Mr. Frisbie's back door. I knew I was being silly. But a curse was a curse, and I didn't want it to rub off on me.

Chapter 9

The next few days were thoughtful ones for me.

I thought a lot about life and death. It seemed strange that the kitten was buried out in the back alley, that it would become bones, that it would never romp and play. I thought about how it would be if I were to die and never again see the sun come up over the tall city buildings. I'd never again smell the warm bread pretzels sold by the old crippled man who waited outside school each noon or feel the furry touch of the monkey's hand in the park on a Saturday afternoon when I handed it a penny and the organ grinder made it tip its hat. Rico must have been thinking thoughts a little like mine because he was unusually sweet to everyone for maybe two whole days.

I thought a lot about my book, too, and I couldn't bring myself to write a word. I had planned out long ago how Joe would die. He would be a hero, sacrificing himself to save a whole battalion of men from a machine gun nest. It didn't matter that I stole the scene from a war movie I had seen.

But the dead kitten had made death a very personal thing to me. It was hard to lose someone you loved, even when you were a mother cat. How could I kill off Joe? How could I make Cynthia suffer? In the end I decided perhaps Joe could still be a hero but maybe be badly wounded and survive. That way Cynthia could suffer, but not so much.

The brooding didn't last too long. It was spring and I was twelve. In the afternoons sometimes Billy let me borrow his skates, and I would go up to the schoolground and fly round and round on the pavement. I learned to skate backwards and only fell down twice. The magnificent feeling of accomplishment more than made up for my skinned knees.

Within a week after the rat episode, Mr. Frisbie tripped on a roller skate left on the front lawn steps. It took three neighborhood men to get him up and into his apartment. "A wrenched back," the doctor announced, and prescribed a week in bed.

Ordinarily if someone was down in bed on our

block, the neighbors would take in food and clean up the apartment. But Mr. Frisbie had been a bear too long. Too many mothers had had their children's bottoms smacked by Mr. Frisbie for trespassing. Mr. Frisbie had to suffer in silence, except for my mother who made him a pot of soup and came away sorry for her kindness.

"Rico left that skate on the steps," Mr. Frisbie told her hotly.

"Rico turned his skates in to the war effort," my mother retorted.

"That Mr. Frisbie," she ranted, telling me about his rudeness. "No wonder he's never found a woman to marry him. As Mrs. DeBasco says, who'd want him?"

"How about that?" some of the neighbors remarked, hearing about Mr. Frisbie's accident. "Rico's curse is working."

Rico had become an object of interest for the whole neighborhood. People would point him out and say, "There goes the brave boy who tried to sit up all night in the alley with his cat friends." And then they would add, "He's the one who put the curse on Mr. Frisbie."

It was all good fun. Nobody really believed in the curse. But when an ancient pipe burst in Mr. Frisbie's kitchen and flooded his apartment and he had to pay plumbers and a mop-up crew because he couldn't get out of bed, everyone said knowingly, "Rico's curse."

People who had never known Rico knew him now. He and Molly became familiar figures on the street. Twice a day he went across to the bakery and got her out of her box and took her for a long walk. She followed him like a dog.

It became apparent that Molly was a one-boy cat. She would allow other children to stroke her now and then, but she never purred for anyone except Rico or rubbed herself against anyone else's legs or permitted anyone else to pick her up.

She was more generous, however, with her kittens, who began to show their own personalities. The calico was quiet and sweet. One of the orange kittens was wild and learned to play before the others. The other was in between, by turns sweet and loving, at other times playing so fiercely she left teeth and claw marks on our hands.

Harold inspected the three kittens and announced

that Rico was right. They were all girls. "And Timothy probably *was* a boy," he said wryly.

"When was Rico ever wrong?" I asked myself.

Days went by, and the kittens became beautiful little fluff balls. Every evening Rico gathered the whole family up and carried them out to the alley. Kids would gather to watch Molly teach her children to hunt.

She found bits of paper for them and spent hours tossing the bits into the air, teasing her children. They learned to crouch and to wiggle their hind ends into springing position. She taught them to soar high into the air after a wafting piece of paper and bat it down with needle-sharp claws.

"One of these days those bits of paper will become birds," Mr. Anastas told Rico. "But then a cat's gotta live. These are city cats. Their mama, she is teaching them to survive in the city."

The kittens learned to hide behind rocks, behind pieces of scrubby bush, underneath newspapers. Molly would walk by them, dragging an old rag. First would come the crouch, then the wriggling in the hind end. Three pink noses would poke out of three different hiding places, twitching and sniffing.

Three pairs of round eyes with black centers would watch and then suddenly pounce.

After a day's lessons, Molly always washed each baby down, her pink tongue rough, her eyes slitted shut. Then Rico would take them all back to the bakery.

"Molly's a good mouser," Mrs. Hall said. "The manager says we can keep her here. If the kittens turn out to be as good, we'll keep them too."

"How much is he going to pay?" Rico demanded. "A good mouser should get paid."

"Well, of all the nerve," Mrs. Hall sputtered. "After I found those homeless kittens a home."

"Well . . ." Rico backed down.

"Tell you what," Mrs. Hall said more kindly. "You're right. Cats do save a bakery a lot of money in losses. Mice get into the flour and other supplies, and once they do, the whole caboodle has to be thrown out. Suppose you come to the bakery every Saturday morning after Molly's walk, and I'll give you a dozen of those chocolate cupcakes you like with the icing on top."

"Hot from the oven?" Rico asked.

"Hot from the oven," she said.

From then on, every Saturday morning a crowd gathered around the bakery door where Rico sold the five-cent cupcakes for seven cents because people liked them hot from the oven. He always bought savings stamps with half the money.

Mr. Frisbie had been up a month when trouble struck again. A gasoline truck overturned on a highway a couple of blocks from our home and exploded. Luckily, the driver got away from his burning truck, and no one was hurt except for a few cuts. On our block only one window was blown out—Mr. Frisbie's.

"Rico's curse," people said again. In Rico's bed I found a little doll made of rags with a pin sticking in its head. "It's a voodoo doll," Rico explained, after he got over being mad at my snooping. "I saw it in a movie. I'm giving Mr. Frisbie headaches."

"For goodness' sake, Rico," I exclaimed. He scared me a little. A week later when I fell down and sprained my wrist, I wondered if Rico didn't have a voodoo doll for me. But I was too afraid to ask.

Chapter 10

Near-summer heat moved into the city. Some days the humidity from the river was so heavy we could hardly stand it. On those days we played quiet games of store in the basement, selling each other pieces of jewelry borrowed from our mothers for play money.

The war news was not good. The Japanese were spunky fighters, and Hitler's armies made bloody paths across Europe. People sang, "When Johnny Comes Marching Home Again, Hurrah, Hurrah."

The last week in May Mr. Alpert died. He had not been taking his walks for a long time before. For days neighbors had been going in and out of the apartment to help care for him. He was simply old, the doctor said. His heart had grown too tired to keep working, and one night it just stopped beating.

I did not hear Mrs. Alpert's words when her husband died. But one of the neighbor women reported them. "Is the last battle over?" she asked. "Is the old soldier gone then?"

Mr. Anastas announced that Mr. Alpert had had a drop of Greek blood and must have a wake. He said that no self-respecting Greek should have his spirit walk alone to the other side of the pale, whatever that meant. Mr. Anastas took charge, and that evening all the neighbors gathered for the event. Billy Loomis's father, who owned a tavern across the street near the bakery, made countless trips to our apartment building, carrying great jugs of wine and pails of beer. Tray after tray of food was carried in, heaping mounds of fancy salads and plates of salami and cheese from a delicatessen and bowls of potato chips and loaves of homemade bread steaming beneath dishtowels. Mrs. Hall brought a day-old cake from the bakery that said, "Happy Birthday Carl."

Soon our building filled up with music. Mr. Anastas had a funny-looking little instrument from the old country that was rather like a small accordion. Mrs. DeBasco's husband brought an organ that had once belonged to an organ grinder before his monkey had died, forcing him to go to work in a factory.

Mrs. Alpert's tiny apartment could not hold all the guests, and they spilled over into the hallway and sat on the steps, praising the departed in several foreign languages.

Outside, the neighborhood kids gathered to listen to the merriment. "Mr. Alpert's body is in there," an awed whisper went through the crowd.

Harold arrived, for he had been a friend of Mr. Alpert's even though the old man and his wife lived in the past. Boys and girls fell upon him. "What's a wake, Harold?" we asked.

"A wake is exactly what it sounds like," he explained. "In many countries, when a person dies, people believe that they must stay up all night with the body until the person's spirit can find its way through the darkness of the outer world we cannot see. These people do not believe death is a time for great grief. They believe that the dead person has left a life of hardship and pain and sorrow and that now at last he will meet all his long-ago friends and relatives. So they sing happy songs and wish his spirit well."

84

Harold smiled and started for the door. "Aren't you coming to the wake, Dee? Your mother said the children in your apartment building were invited."

I shrank back and bumped into Marilyn, who had also been invited. "Mr. Alpert's still in there," I said in horror.

"Not really Mr. Alpert," Harold said gently. "Only his earthly remains." But I shook my head. Harold shrugged and pushed on through the doors.

I was dying to go but didn't have the nerve. Of course, Rico went, and I hated him for it. Not only did Rico go, but he took Molly too. "Molly's never been to a wake," he announced, coming from the bakery with the cat in his arms.

The wake roared on late into the night. Parents forgot to send their children home, and we sat about, bone-tired but fascinated. Once Mr. DeBasco came outside and said, "If the children cannot come to the wake, the wake will come to the children." He carried a candle in a holder, which he placed on the ground beside him, and then he played a rousing, squeaky song on the organ grinder's organ.

Harold brought out a tray full of cake, and I got a piece of the word *Carl.* Toward midnight Rico came weaving down the steps through the merrymakers and said in a slurred voice, "I'm taking Molly back to the bakery. People fed her too much wine." He set the cat down, and she wobbled about a moment with a silly look on her face, and then her legs simply went out from under her and she splatted down to the ground on her stomach.

"That is a fine cat," Mr. Anastas said, on his way across the street to order more wine. "But a little drunk."

"So is Rico," I added.

"Of course," said Mr. Anastas. "Though he drank only a glass or two of wine. It is customary for children to drink wine at important events like wakes."

"How does Mr. Alpert look?" Marilyn demanded in a hushed voice.

"Like Mr. Alpert," Rico said. "Who else? He's wearing his Sunday suit, and he's smiling, and bandles are curning all around his bed."

"Bandles?" someone muttered. "Are curning?"

The wake went on all that night. My parents came outside to check on me and found at least twenty children still gathered and knew I was safe and went back inside. Some of my friends fell asleep on the stoop.

Dawn came slowly over the city. I woke from a doze to find people going home at last. "It was a fine wake," Mr. Anastas said. His shirt was unbuttoned down the front, and he had broken his little accordion, but he looked happy. "The hearse is coming at eight," he said. "I am going home now to dress myself up."

"Come on to bed, Dee," my father said wearily.

"After the hearse," I said. Dawn had brought a cool dampness that was refreshing after the long, loud night, and I didn't feel tired at all.

Promptly at eight o'clock, a long black car slid to the curb in front of our building. All the children who were left stood there respectfully, a little excited, and a little scared. A hearse had never stopped on our block before.

The wake guests returned, somewhat sober now, dressed in good clothes, to stand in two long lines beside the sidewalk. Four men got out of the hearse and carried a huge black coffin inside the house. We fell back a little then, for most of us had never seen a coffin.

In only moments we watched through the glass doors as the men and my father and Mr. Anastas and Mr. DeBasco and Rico carried the coffin back outside. My mother followed, helping Mrs. Alpert who looked more ancient and wrinkled than ever before. Mrs. Alpert wore a black veil hanging from her hat and down her back.

We watched in silence as the huge doors of the hearse swung open, and the coffin was placed inside. "Goodbye," people called. "Goodbye, Mr. Alpert." There were a few tears and some sniffles, then the doors swung shut.

"The war is over," Mrs. Alpert said to no one in particular. The hearse moved quietly away from the curb with no sound at all from its big motor.

Some people shook hands with Mrs. Alpert and then went slowly away. In the doorway of our building, Mr. Frisbie stood with a sour look on his face. He had not come out of his apartment all night, but he had not tried to stop the wake, either.

I think I was the only one looking at him when the hearse pulled away. I caught something strange in his face that surprised me. It was a kind of sadness, a pain. And then it was gone and the sourness was back.

Puzzled, I turned away.

I forgot Mr. Frisbie, for my mother was leading Mrs. Alpert back to her apartment. The old woman did not look as if she knew any of us.

I went upstairs and took a nap, and when I came back downstairs a few hours later, there was another strange car at the curb. My mother came out of Mrs. Alpert's apartment with a man and woman who were leading Mrs. Alpert between them. She still wore that dazed look.

"Mrs. Alpert is going away to live with distant relatives, dear," my mother explained, when she saw my puzzlement. "She is very old and very tired, and it is a great shock to lose the man to whom you've been married for nearly sixty years. She won't be able to take care of herself. But perhaps she'll come back and see us one day."

As the car pulled away from the curb, I felt tears sting my throat. I knew I would never again hear Mrs. Alpert singing the songs of a long-ended war.

Chapter 11

I was tired, but I didn't want to go back to bed. I wanted to be on the streets, listening to the city. There was hardly anyone playing on our section of the block; the wake had tired everyone out.

But I took a walk. Up to the school, around the corner, down the next street, past the haunted house. I didn't even look at it, although my steps quickened automatically. A little farther on, a dog behind a screen door barked at me.

I watched my black and white saddle oxfords scuffle along the sidewalk, listened to the pluffing sound. When I was very little, my kindergarten class had held a parade along this sidewalk. The parade was to call attention to Clean-Up Week in the city, and the girls had worn little white paper maids' caps and aprons and carried brooms. I had been so proud of myself in my costume.

Now for some reason I thought of Mrs. Alpert, and I wished I was that little girl again. I didn't want to get any older.

There was a bright sun over the city. Someone was practicing a trumpet someplace, and I listened to the sour notes and smiled. A tree that had been bare all winter thrust a green-leafed branch in front of my face as if to say, "How can you be gloomy?"

All of a sudden Billy Loomis came flying around the block on his bicycle. He saw me and skidded to a stop. "You up, too? Come on! I'll give you a ride." I got on behind him, and as we rode wildly off, old age suddenly seemed a million suns away.

Rico slept all that day, and for the first time he forgot to feed Molly. It wasn't until pink evening had settled over the city that he roused himself and went across the street to the bakery. His feet dragged, and there were dark circles under his eyes.

Minutes later he came tearing wild-eyed out of the building. "Molly's gone!" he hollered.

Mrs. Hall followed him, a worried look on her round face. Rico whirled on her in a fury. "How come you didn't tell me?" he cried.

Taken aback, it was a second before Mrs. Hall responded, "You must have the meanest mouth I know, Rico Haymacher."

"I'm sorry, Mrs. Hall," Rico said unexpectedly. Rico never apologized to anybody unless Mama held him by the collar and made him. "I'm just worried."

All evening while the other kids charged about the streets playing ball, Rico sat on the front stoop with his chin in his hands, watching for Molly to come back.

"Jeez, he gives me the creeps," Jimmy blurted out once. "He ain't even blinking."

Mr. Frisbie came out the door with a broom and swept the stoop all around Rico. Rico coughed, but he didn't move, and for some strange reason Mr. Frisbie didn't make him. I suspected that Mr. Frisbie was beginning to believe Rico's curse.

My father nearly had to drag Rico up to the apartment, and even then he insisted on sleeping on the sofa.

"I don't want to upset you, dear," my mother said. "But we'd better accept the fact that Molly might have gone away. Often mother cats do leave their families, you know—when the children are old enough to care for themselves. After all, Molly *is* a city cat. She may have simply moved on."

"Molly wouldn't leave *me*," Rico muttered. "And she was drunk. Somebody probably let her out the bakery door, and she got lost."

All that night he sat on the sofa, his eyes watching the bakery from our front window. Toward morning he woke up, hating himself for falling asleep, and tore across the street to see if she had come home. I followed and my fears came true. Molly had not returned.

"Would you believe one of those little orange devils caught a baby mouse this morning?" one of the bakers said admiringly. Any other time Rico would have been proud, but now he only went dejectedly home to get ready for school.

We were just coming onto the school playground when Sally Hall came screaming down the back alley and through the place in the school fence where a slat was missing.

"I saw her, I saw her!" Sally shrieked. "The Mad Scientist's got Molly!"

"You're crazy!" Rico shouted into her face. But all that could be gotten out of Sally was, "I saw her. I saw her in the window!"

In moments Rico had organized a war party of third-graders. Armed with sticks and rocks and terrified eyes, they marched through the slat and up the alley. Some of the older kids trudged along behind, scared but fascinated. "What are you going to do if she *is* in there?" I yelled to Rico.

"Send you in after her," he said with a sneer.

In another minute the third-graders were lined up in battle formation. "I don't see Molly in that window," somebody whispered.

"I don't see the Mad Scientist either," another voice answered.

"We'll know in a minute," Rico said. Then he stomped down the line of warriors like a general and whispered something to each one. A second later he raised his stick high and then let his hand drop. In unison the third-graders started yelling, "Kitty, kitty, kitty. Here, kitty, kitty, kitty." Rico's voice rose above the others, keeping rhythm.

Suddenly, something leaped into the window of the Mad Scientist's laboratory. We fell back through the fence.

"It's Molly!" Rico shouted in dismay. "It really is. He's got her trapped."

94

And then the unbelievable happened. For just an instant a face appeared at the window above Molly's form. "Help!" Sally screamed.

A horde of kids trampled each other, running back to the playground. I was one of the first back and Rico was right behind me. Others raced to join us. "The Mad Scientist, the Mad Scientist!" everybody jabbered at once.

Rico's teacher, Miss Limkin, arrived with Mr. Bodgewell. "What in the world is all this noise?" Miss Limkin demanded.

"The Mad Scientist's got Molly the cat," we chorused.

"Nonsense," Mr. Bodgewell said. He turned to Miss Limkin. "I have had my fill of this foolishness." he said. "The children have seen far too many monster movies. I am going into my office to call the authorities and insist that they bring out a search warrant for that old building. Once and for all I shall prove to these children that there *is* no Mad Scientist."

"You'll be sorry," Jimmy mumbled. He seemed to have forgotten his father had said there was no Mad Scientist. "He'll put your brain in an ape."

Mr. Bodgewell turned level eyes on Jimmy. "You, Master Grossinger," he said, "will keep quiet. You are merely inciting the younger children to riot. Miss Limkin, you will restore order, please, while I make my phone call."

"You children break it up," Miss Limkin said, as Mr. Bodgewell strode back toward the building. "The bell will ring in ten minutes."

"I'm going in there *now,*" Rico said suddenly. "Before the Mad Scientist turns Molly into something."

"What did you say?" I gasped, as he made his way back through the slat. For a long moment I just stood there with my mouth hanging open. Then I got my senses back and ran for Miss Limkin, who had begun to herd children toward the school. "Miss Limkin, Miss Limkin!" I called. "Rico's gone into the laboratory after Molly."

"Oh, good grief," Miss Limkin muttered. She walked back to peer through the fence. "Rico Haymacher, you come right back here!" But Rico had already done the unbelievable thing. He had stepped into the overgrown yard that surrounded the Mad Scientist's laboratory.

Chapter 12

We all stared after Rico. "He'll be killed," someone cried.

"I don't want Rico to be a monster," one of his buddies yelled. "He might eat me!"

Determined, Miss Limkin went through the fence, and one by one, at least forty children followed close behind her. Not one of us meant to advance a step past Miss Limkin's thin form.

"Rico Haymacher"—she threatened him—"you're going to get a spanking from Mr. Bodgewell."

"Are you going in after him, Miss Limkin?" Tommy Mitchell, another of Rico's buddies, asked.

Miss Limkin's eyes went to the dirty window where we had seen Molly and the Mad Scientist. "If I must." She sighed. "But I am not fond of exploring dark places probably full of loose boards."

How brave she is, I thought. Then suddenly we

heard the sound of a door creaking open, and we knew Rico had reached the front of the building and had pushed open the ancient door. Miss Limkin started forward. She was actually going *in* there. Fascinated, I stared at her with admiration, proud of her courage. But she was going to be too late, for I knew I would never again see my brother—at least not as I had always known him. He was a brat, but I didn't want him turned into a monster by the Mad Scientist.

Miss Limkin picked her way across old hunks of wood and fallen tree branches. Before she had advanced very far, there came a long, horrible screech. Miss Limkin stopped dead in her tracks. The hair raised up on the back of my neck. "That's Rico!" I shouted.

Before any of us could get our jellied legs stiff enough to run, a streak tore around the side of the laboratory and ran for us. "Japs, Japs!" Rico bellowed. "Call the army. Call an airplane!"

He crashed headlong into Miss Limkin. "Hey, he's got Molly," somebody shouted.

"Japs!" Rico shrieked. "Miss Limkin, there's Japs in there." He tore on past her and reached us.

Miss Limkin followed him back through the fence. "Rico, make sense," she snapped.

Above the sound of excitement, a new noise arrived. Up the alley, bouncing along the ruts, tore a squad car. Two big men got out and came toward us. "Okay, people," one of them said. "What's up? We've had a dozen calls complaining about the noise." He looked to Miss Limkin for help.

"The children's imaginations . . ." she began.

"Rico just saved Molly from the Mad Jap," Sally babbled.

"No, no! From the Mad Scientist," Tommy cried.

"It isn't a Mad Scientist," Rico shouted. "It's Japs. The place is full of Japs. Call a tank!"

In the end, when Miss Limkin had managed to sort out the wild tale above the jabbering voices, the policemen announced they would go into the building and dig out the problem.

"They'll ambush you," Rico warned. "My cat and me barely got out alive."

"Are there really Japs in there?" I whispered in shock, as the policemen headed through the weeds.

"Hundreds," Rico insisted. "They probably

sneaked in on subs up the Mississippi to blow up our bridges and things."

"How could so many of them get here on subs without being spotted?" I asked.

"Shut up," Rico said disgustedly, the way he always did when he was stumped. "I hope they torture you."

It seemed a year, but it couldn't have been more than a few minutes before the officers were back. At the sight of a man walking between the two policemen, half the crowd dashed away screaming, "The Mad Scientist!"

"It doesn't look much like a Mad Scientist to me," Miss Limkin said. "It looks more like a frightened old man. But you're right, Rico. He *is* Japanese."

"It's the darndest thing," one of the officers said, when they reached Miss Limkin's side. "Looks like he's been living there weeks maybe. He's got a little makeshift stove he's been burning sticks in."

"And a bed made out of rags," the other added.

The brave ones among us crowded behind Miss Limkin to get a closer look.

"Who is he?" somebody asked.

"Beats me," the policeman mumbled. "He doesn't seem to speak any English." For a long time we all just stood there, staring at the little man with the yellow-brown skin and slanted eyes.

"Is he a spy?" I asked timidly.

"He's too old to be a spy," the officer said. "Seventy, if he's a day. Eighty, maybe."

The old man's eyes went to Molly in Rico's arms. They clouded with tears and suddenly, to my surprise, Rico, who had gone strangely calm at the sight of his "hundreds of Japs," held out the cat to him. Molly, who usually didn't want anything to do with anybody but Rico, went right into the old man's arms. He held her against his cheek, and tears ran down his wrinkled face.

At last they put the old man in the squad car in the back seat. As he was climbing in, he handed the cat back to Rico and said something in a language we could not understand. He was still crying when the squad car pulled away. Miss Limkin had tears in her eyes, too. So did I, though I couldn't have told you why.

That night my father called the police to find out about the old man. "His family reported him missing weeks ago," the sergeant on duty told him. "He's been brooding a long time about the way Japanese in California and other western states were taken from their homes and put into camps. He feels he's a loyal American, and he was terrified he might be sent to a camp."

My father was quiet when he came away from the phone. Harold had heard of the day's excitement, and he stopped in to get the story firsthand. He told Rico and me about what were called internment camps.

. That was the first time I had heard about the West Coast Japanese. I didn't know that whole groups of them had been sent to camps all surrounded with barbed wire. The government thought it was protecting us, I suppose, from spies and American Japanese who might be loyal to the Emperor of Japan. But Harold said children and babies who couldn't possibly be spies were put in the camps, too. That night I lay awake a long, long time thinking of those babies shut up behind barbed wire.

Chapter 13

In the morning Rico announced that he would not be going to school until noon. "Why not?" my mother asked, shocked.

"Because I'm taking something to that old Japanese man," he said. "Daddy's going to drive me."

"When did he say that?" my mother demanded.

"I didn't tell him yet," Rico said. "But he will."

And he did. He took me, too, because he thought it was a fine thing for Rico to do. My mother rode along.

We drove to the old district in the city, near the waterfront. At last we found a little restaurant that said, "CHINESE FOOD." The word Japanese had been crossed out and replaced by the word Chinese.

The restaurant wasn't open yet, and we all got out of the car and walked around to the back where there was an apartment. My father knocked on the door, and a young woman answered. She had yellow-brown skin and black eyes.

"We've come with a gift for your grandfather," my father said, and we explained who we were. She smiled and stood aside for us to pass.

The old man was sitting in a chair by a table with a pot of tea in front of him. When he saw Rico, he looked pleased and a little bit frightened.

Without a word, Rico walked to him and placed his gift in his lap. For a long time the old man just stared down at the bundle of orange fluff. "She's a good mouser," Rico said. "She's already caught a baby mouse."

The young woman spoke rapidly to the old man in Japanese, and his smile widened. He picked up the kitten and held her against his cheek. *"Arigato,"* he said, and even I understood his thanks.

The young woman insisted we come into the restaurant, which was decorated in orange and black with paper lanterns hanging from the ceiling. She turned on a lightswitch, and the lanterns lit up, and they looked so pretty that I gasped.

Then she sat us down at a table. The old man joined us carrying his kitten, her husband came in

with a fat little baby who made me think of those other babies in California. We had a fine breakfast of something I'd never tasted before. "It's really a Japanese dish," the young woman explained. "But we call it Ming Chow Mein now because that's Chinese. Nobody would want to come to a Japanese restaurant while the war is on."

Little by little we discovered what had taken place in that barn. Molly had wandered out, still slightly drunk, on the night of the wake. She was used to prowling the alley for a little while and then going back to the bakery to wait for somebody to let her in. But on this night, a little dazed in the head, she had roamed too far, into the backyard of the old barn.

A fine brown mouse had run in front of her, and she had chased it into the building. The old man told us that, and his granddaughter translated his words. He had caught Molly and wanted to keep her with him because he was lonesome. The mystery of who had been robbing a lot of the Victory gardens in the neighborhood at night was solved too. The old man had been living on vegetables patriotically grown so that farmers could send more of their crops for the army to eat.

"We will go to those houses and explain and pay them back," his granddaughter said. "He is not a thief. He was only frightened." People of Japanese ancestry had not been so badly treated in this city, she told us. But relatives of theirs had been sent to a California camp called Manzanar. "They are loyal Americans," she said. "But they are not trusted. This is why my grandfather was afraid."

At last we all shook hands with everybody, and Mr. Nakamura (that was the Mad Scientist's name) begged us to come back again. "Everyone has been so kind," his granddaughter said. "I think he understands now that everyone knows he is a loyal American."

As if he understood, the old man went to a drawer and came back and pressed something into Rico's hands. It was a tiny American flag.

At noon Rico and I went back to school, past the old barn where a blank window stared down into the alley. I knew that was the end of *that* Mad Scientist, at least until somebody made up a new one.

Chapter 14

The next morning when he came to the breakfast table, Rico announced angrily, "I don't like the war anymore. It's no fun."

"Wars aren't supposed to be fun," my father said.

"Sure they are," Rico insisted. "The paper drives used to be fun. The scrap drives were fun. Saving stamps was fun. It used to be fun to go to the store with Mama and fight with Nick the Butcher when he tried to cheat her out of meat ration stamps."

On and on Rico ranted, his voice going up and up, and pretty soon he was banging his fork on the table, and little bits of eggs were splattering everyplace.

"Tinfoil's no fun, either," Rico snorted. Every kid in school had a tinfoil ball, big shiny globs made up of the insides of cigarette and gum wrappers. I'm not sure what the army wanted tinfoil for, maybe to help make bullets. Rico had made the biggest ball on our block.

"I'm going to write President Roosevelt and tell him to stop this dumb war," Rico declared.

"That's a fine attitude, son," my father said with a small grin. "But what makes you think Mr. Roosevelt isn't doing everything in his power to stop the war anyway? How would you suggest he get it stopped?"

"Just stop fighting," Rico said fiercely.

"What about our enemies, Rico? What if they don't want to stop? What if they just keep on fighting and killing our men anyway and then come over and bomb us too?"

For a long time Rico stared at the eggs he'd messed around in his plate. "Well, shoot," he said. When he raised his eyes, I was surprised to see tears in them. "I didn't know the Japs were people before. Maybe they don't all want to have a war with us. Maybe kids like me don't want to fight anybody."

"Or mothers," Mama put in sadly. "Mothers don't want to fight anybody either."

"You're quite a boy, Rico Haymacher," my father

said. "Sometimes you seem a lot older than your years."

For days after that Rico went around in a dejected state. Ever since the war started, Rico had been working hard to make bullets and cannons and airplanes. Now he just sat in glum silence out in the alley in his fort, his chin on his knees. Even his buddies didn't know quite what to do with him. Rico had always been their leader, and without his winning-the-war ideas, they were lost. One day I found him in the alley shredding up his tinfoil ball and tossing the little pieces into the ashpit.

"For goodness' sake!" I shrieked. "That would have made a hundred bullets anyway."

"I don't want to make any bullets," he shouted. "Bullets kill people."

I thought about that a while, and then I went upstairs and tore up my own tinfoil ball. Putting the pieces in a paper sack, I went down to drop it in the ashpit.

Kids were playing up and down the alley. Staring toward the Mad Scientist's former lair, I felt a little sad. Some Mad Scientist! I was not going to forget how Mr. Nakamura had looked coming out of his "laboratory." I watched a flock of sparrows settle on the roof of the old barn. That was all it seemed like now, an old brick barn.

"Ah-ee-ah-ee-ah!" someone screamed. It was a little redheaded Tarzan swinging from a rope hanging from a dead alley tree. The sweet smell from the bakery hung over the neighborhood. "Fresh fish!" a gruff voice shouted down the street. The birds took off again and dropped to sit chattering on electric wires at the side of our building.

"Are there birds at Manzanar?" I wondered. I thought of the fences holding all those Japanese children. Suddenly I wanted to rush out and wrap the whole alley, the whole neighborhood, the whole city in my arms. If I could have, I would have carried it all out to Manzanar.

Later that afternoon Rico found me in our room hard at work on a class project. He stuck his head in the door and grunted and turned away. Then he changed his mind and came hopping curiously into the room.

"What's that you got?" he asked.

I stared down at the ugly, khaki-colored yarn in my hands. "It's a blanket I'm making," I said.

"Miss Sheehan got the yarn someplace. The Red Cross, I think."

Rico's eyes narrowed. "What's the blanket for?" he demanded.

"For a soldier," I said. "I make a whole bunch of little squares and sew them together and then it gets sent off to the army. Everybody in my class is making things. Scarves, too. And hats. For wearing in trenches. Even though it isn't summer yet, winter will be here before we know it, Miss Sheehan says, and our boys will need these things."

"How come that square is all full of holes?"

"Well, I made a little mistake here and there," I mumbled.

"I could knit better than that with my eyes closed," Rico snorted. "If I wanted to, that is. Boys don't knit."

"Boys in my class do," I said huffily. I looked at my square. It wasn't too bad. After all, it was my first one. I'd only learned to knit recently, and I had only dropped nine stitches so far.

"I never saw a boy knit," Rico sniffed.

"Well, they're knitting in my class, you little brat," I shouted into his face. "Miss Sheehan says it's nothing to be ashamed of. Miss Sheehan says it's important to keep our boys warm."

Rico looked thoughtful, but he didn't say any more. That night I found him huddled on his bed all tangled up in a bunch of red yarn. He had two knitting needles in his hands, and he was jabbing them in and out of the yarn.

"What are you doing?" I asked.

"Practicing," he said. "Mama showed me how. Listen, you get me some yarn from your class and I'll make things too. Only if you tell anybody, I'll put a curse on you just like I did on Mr. Frisbie. I'll make all your hair fall out."

"You wouldn't," I gasped.

"You want to see me try?" he demanded, with a mean look in his eyes.

The next day I brought Rico home a whole gob of yarn. "How come you're doing this?" I asked. "Instead of collecting things?"

"Well," he said soberly. "I want the war to get over, but I don't want to hurt anybody."

Rico's first square had fifteen dropped stitches, but I was afraid if I laughed he'd put that curse on me. Not that I *really* believed he could do it, of course.

Rico had made three squares when he decided knitting a blanket was boring. "I want to make socks," he said.

"Ha!" I cried. "That's for advanced people. You have to knit on four needles. Even Mama doesn't know how."

That didn't stop Rico. "Miss Sheehan can help me," he said. "I don't care if *she* knows I'm knitting."

How could Rico know that two of his buddies would watch him go into my classroom one day after school? They peeked through the door while Rico was intent on learning how to handle four needles. I had stayed to learn, too, so I was there when the two little boys fell over on the hall floor, screaming and laughing.

"Hey, Miss Rico," one of them shouted. "Wait'll the guys hear this!"

My brother got off his chair, very carefully laid down his knitting, and then marched out the door and hauled both his buddies to their feet and punched them. "I'm helping our boys at the front," he declared. "You want to make something out of it?"

"Bring your friends in," Miss Sheehan said. "Per-

haps I can reassure them that knitting is not a sissy job. It's very important. Anybody can gather scrap. Not everyone can knit."

In the morning Rico went off to school carrying his knitting right out in the open. That afternoon, a whole horde of boys, glad to be doing something again, sat around in our yard biting their lips and casting on stitches. "Men with cold feet can't get wars over with," Rico explained to any adult who caught him knitting. Just in case anybody thought to laugh.

The socks were marvelous to see. Rico's pair was the strangest of all. One sock would scarcely fit my doll Brunhilda, and an elephant could easily have gotten a foot in the other. But Rico didn't care. He thought they were beautiful and started on a second pair. Late into the evening, after everyone else had gone home, he would sit knitting in the alley just outside our backyard while Molly and her two remaining kittens, who were fast growing up, romped around.

"If that cat comes in my yard, I'll shoot her," Mr. Frisbie bellowed at least once an evening. But Molly seemed to know her boundaries and only once raised her nose to sniff disdainfully at Mr. Frisbie.

Days went by. A new couple moved into the Alpert's old apartment. Nobody ever saw them because they both worked long hours in a war plant and they didn't have any children.

Then one day Harold stopped by our apartment, and he had a whole new idea for Rico. "Listen," he said. "I got a V-mail letter from a friend stationed near a little town in England. I don't know the name because the censors wouldn't have let him write it. But he's worried about all the townspeople, especially the babies. They've suffered heavy bombing, and most of their belongings have been destroyed. They need food and clothing. What would you say to a little clothing drive? I could mail the things to my friend's APO number in New York, and he could give them to the people over there."

"We'll start tomorrow!" Rico cried.

The next morning was Saturday, and Rico sent buddies running to gather every boy they could find. When everybody was gathered, which meant what looked like a million boys swarming all over the alley, Rico got on an orange crate in his fort and shouted out his news about our allies in the English town.

"We're going to personally save them!" he shouted.

"Yay!" screeched his followers.

"Mr. Frisbie won't let us use his yard, so we'll stack all the clothes in Louie's yard till Harold helps us pack them."

"Yay, yay!"

Rico wound up his speech by leading a rousing chorus of "When the lights go on again all over the world," and all the screaming little boys went tearing off, thrilled to be on a drive again. "We need baby clothes especially," Rico shouted after them.

In spite of myself, my heart was pounding after Rico's glorious speech on behalf of clothesless babies. "What can I do?" I cried.

"Go back to your knitting," he said disdainfully. "That's all girls are good for in wars." He started off to join his buddies.

"You knit too!" I shouted after him.

"But that's not *all* I can do," he hollered back. As always, I stood there smarting with anger. Someday when no one was looking, I might kill that little brat. In the meantime I wasn't about to be stopped. I gathered Marilyn and some other girls, and we went collecting too.

By dusk Louie Loomis's small yard was full of boxes of clothing. Even Mrs. DeBasco, who hadn't yet donated a thing to any drive, was so overcome when Rico and four other boys stood in the hallway outside her apartment and sang *"God Save the Queen,"* that she dragged out her old winter coat for them.

"What are you going to give, Rico?" I demanded at dinner. "You don't have any old clothes, especially baby stuff." I found out soon enough, and in a very odd way, what Rico meant to contribute.

A few days later, Rico and his buddies had finished their clothing drive, and Harold had promised to help them box everything up over the weekend.

"The boys in England are going to be so happy," he told Rico and his gang. "You're saving some lives, you know. English winters can be very severe."

Until this Wednesday night I had practically forgotten all about Rico's curse on Mr. Frisbie. After all, nothing much new had happened to Mr. Frisbie. He stayed out of our way so much we hardly saw him.

Rico went to bed early, exhausted by his latest

patriotic effort. I was in the bathtub, which was a bad place to be at that moment. When I first heard Mr. Frisbie's terrified voice shouting, "Helphelpfire-help!" I thought it was only a kid goofing off in the street. Then suddenly my father was knocking on the bathroom door and saying in a quiet but urgent voice, "Get out of the tub, Dee. Dress quickly. The building is on fire."

Chapter 15

It is not easy to dress when you are soaking wet and covered with soap besides. But I got into the dress I'd thrown on the floor and raced wildly into the living room. My mother was too upset even to holler at my dripping on the rug.

My father had Rico on his feet, shaking him awake. "Rico," he said swiftly. "Would you go with your mother and sister downstairs, please? I'm going to make sure the Hall children are out."

I couldn't believe the building was on fire, despite the way Mr. Frisbie's voice went on bleating somewhere beneath us. But when we opened the door to the hallway, smoke billowed up the stairs and rushed around us. My eyes began to sting fiercely, and I couldn't see a thing.

"Take my hand, Dee," Rico said. "I'll lead you." A little surprised, but grateful to have another human being to hang onto, I let him lead me down the steps, groping one foot at a time. Mama came behind, and we could hear the startled voices of Marilyn and Sally as my father led them to safety. By now Mr. Frisbie was in the front yard, running around the way I had seen chickens do after their heads had been wrung off. Smoke poured out of all the basement windows.

A hook-and-ladder fire truck roared up the street, coming in two parts around the corner, and then firemen swarmed through our yard. The neighbors started gathering again. Mrs. Hall came tearing out of the bakery crying, "Save my children!" just like in a movie. When she discovered them safe, she began to weep and went around begging for understanding.

"You understand, don't you, Mr. Anastas?" Mrs. Hall demanded, catching him by the lapels of his blue bathrobe. "I have to work to support my girls. They're old enough to stay alone. But I check them twenty times a night," she told my father. And then she fell into my mother's arms and sobbed, "Everybody hates me. Everybody thinks I neglect my girls."

Firemen plunged in and out of doors and windows and raced up ladders for no reason I could see since the fire was plainly in the basement. A tinge of sadness touched me when I realized Mrs. Alpert wasn't here to enjoy the excitement. She probably would have thought a bomb had fallen.

"What's that white stuff all over you?" Billy demanded. "You look stupid." I stared down at flecks of dried soap.

Mr. Frisbie was in a fit. "My building," he kept moaning. Molly had come out of the bakery with some of the other employees who were standing around watching the fire. Rico picked her up, and Mr. Frisbie stopped his pacing suddenly and pointed a finger at her.

"It's all that cat's fault," he shouted. "All the trouble started when she came. She's a jinx. She brought me bad luck."

"Only black cats bring bad luck," Rico said, hugging Molly protectingly.

"Rico's curse," Jimmy Grossinger said suddenly in an awed voice. "It worked again on Mr. Frisbie." All the neighbors started talking at once about the curse.

Mr. Frisbie poked a finger right up against Molly's nose. "Either that cat leaves the neighborhood tonight, or tomorrow she winds up in the river!" he roared. Then he turned back helplessly to watch streams of water from the fire hoses pouring into the basement.

In a little while the firemen had finished their mad dashing around. The chief was a balding little man with a wet cigar hanging out of his mouth. He fought his way through a bunch of admirers who wanted to touch his slicker. "Can I have your autograph?" Louie Loomis called from somewhere low in the crowd.

"Might have been a wiring fire," the chief said. "In the basement walls. Take a couple of days maybe to pin the cause for sure. Could have been a mouse, maybe, got into some matches left down there. Or . . ."

Mr. Frisbie suddenly shifted all attention to himself. "My clothes!" he screeched suddenly, in a voice that must have carried all the way to Mrs. Alpert, wherever she was. He tore wildly around the side of the house with the chief and two firemen hot behind him.

"Don't go in that house!" the chief hollered. "Be a while before we're sure the smouldering's stopped." Like people at a movie, caught up in the action, the whole crowd surged around to the back yard.

There was no stopping Mr. Frisbie. He plunged through the doorway where the firemen had ripped the screen off its hinges. "My clothes!" we could hear him yelling. The chief rushed in after him.

In a few moments Mr. Frisbie came back. The crowd had been chattering excitedly about this strange new outburst. But now, with one look at his face, everybody fell silent. I don't know how long we stood there with the odd smell of dead fire in our noses, just staring at Mr. Frisbie.

His face wore a blank expression, as if all his thoughts had run away. Then suddenly he sat down hard, right there on the ground outside the screen door. "They're gone," he said. "Everything in my locker's burned up. My clothes are gone. The only thing I had left, and they're gone." A tear rolled down his cheek.

Everyone stared at Mr. Frisbie in shock. Mr. Anastas moved slowly through the crowd to stand above

126

him, a puzzled look in his eyes. He reached out slowly and put a hand on Mr. Frisbie's shoulder. "They're gone," Mr. Frisbie said again. "All I had left."

"What's all the excitement?" somebody asked. I stared up at Harold pushing his way through the crowd. "I was on my way home from the hospital," he said. "I saw the fire trucks."

"Mr. Frisbie is crying, Harold," Rico said. Rico looked the most stunned of all. Still clutching Molly close, he walked over to stand by Mr. Anastas.

"It wasn't really a curse, Mr. Frisbie," he said. "Witches are the only ones that can make curses. But I'll take it away anyway if you want."

Mr. Frisbie just sat there, his hands folded in his lap. "My box of clothes," was all he would say. "Their things. The baby hats and the . . ."

"Baby clothes?" Rico's face lit up as if someone had turned a flashlight on it, but nobody saw that except me. And nobody but me saw him suddenly disappear from the crowd.

Mr. Frisbie still sat there when Rico came tearing through the back gate lugging a cardboard box. Molly trailed along behind him.

"Here's your clothes, Mr. Frisbie," he bellowed. "I knew where they were. They were right on top of the pile from our apartment building." He ran to set the box in front of Mr. Frisbie.

For a long moment Mr. Frisbie didn't seem to understand, and then slowly the truth got through to him. "The clothes?" he cried. "These are my things?" He began to tear through the garments in the box. Then he stopped and held up a frilly pink baby jacket.

My father had filled Harold in on what had happened, and now Harold went to Mr. Frisbie. He took the pink jacket in his hands and stared at it a moment. "Whose was it, Mr. Frisbie?" he asked.

"It belonged to the baby we never had," Mr. Frisbie said quietly. "Sarah and me." His tears had stopped. "My wife, Sarah, made all these things. And there are some of her clothes in here too." He touched a piece of dark material in the box. "I guess we wanted that baby more than anything in the world."

"I didn't know Mr. Frisbie was ever married," Mrs. DeBasco said from somewhere in the crowd. "Who would have suspected?"

"What happened to them, Mr. Frisbie?" Harold asked.

"She died in childbirth," Mr. Frisbie said. "A long time ago."

"I didn't know," Rico said helplessly to nobody in particular. "I thought Mr. Frisbie was just being stingy like always. I knew that box of clothes was down there because I discovered it when Molly borned her kitties. I took them to help the English babies that might get cold this winter. We didn't get too many baby clothes."

"That was wrong, son," my father said angrily. "That was stealing."

"No!" Mr. Frisbie got to his feet. He didn't look the least bit mean all of a sudden. He just looked sort of old and tired. "If Rico hadn't taken the clothes, they would have burned and I wouldn't have anything." He looked helplessly at Harold. "She was the only woman I ever loved," he explained.

Holding the baby jacket close to his chest, Mr. Frisbie turned to Rico. "Thank you for taking my clothes," he said. "I'm grateful."

Rico, always one to take advantage of a situation,

latched onto Mr. Frisbie's gratitude. "Can Molly and her kittens move in with us then?" he demanded. "After everything's fixed up again?"

Mr. Frisbie's eyes sparked just a second. Then he sighed. "All right," he said. "If they stay out of my way."

"Whoopee!" Rico shouted. "Did you hear that, Molly?" He snatched her up and planted a kiss on her pink nose.

Chapter 16

My family spent the night with Harold, all of us sleeping on the floor of his tiny room. Mr. Frisbie went home with Mr. Anastas, and Mrs. DeBasco took the Hall family in. The new couple must have worked all night.

In the morning we all trooped back to the apartment house. Mr. Frisbie already had men working to repair the damage the fire had caused. The fire had been confined to the walls in the basement, and the other floors hadn't been harmed at all. We could move right in again even though the smell of smoke was on everything.

In the afternoon my father, who had stayed home from work to help with cleaning up, found Rico sitting in the front room window. He was staring down at the street.

"What is it, son?" my father asked.

"I was thinking about Mr. Frisbie," Rico said slowly. "How he turned out to be a person just like Mr. Nakamura. I mean—I don't know what I mean."

"I think I do," my father said. "I think you're beginning to realize that Mr. Frisbie was mean because he was terribly unhappy."

"I didn't know he was unhappy," Rico said. "I shouldn't have put a curse on him."

"Well, it's over now," my father said. "I think Mr. Frisbie will be different from now on. He's shared his problem, and I think he really appreciated everyone's concern and understanding. Perhaps no one is ever mean without a reason."

That evening Molly moved in with us, but Rico left her two babies at the bakery to go on catching mice. "They don't need Molly anymore," Rico said. "Besides, she growls at them. I guess she's trying to kick them out of the cat nest."

"You went into the alley again at night," I said to Rico, "to get Mr. Frisbie's clothes from Louie's yard. Weren't you scared?"

"Sure," Rico admitted. "But I go into the alley when I have to."

132

"You're a brat," I said. "But sometimes I love you." I thought he might kick me in the shins, so I dodged, but he only grinned.

"That's because I'm lovable," he said.

Summer came and brought blistering heat to the sidewalks. If we went barefoot, we burned our feet. At the fire station two blocks away, the firemen set up big hoses to spray an area in the street so that we could run and play in cool water. Ice-cream carts filled the sidewalks, and children set up lemonade stands to make money to buy popsicles.

Two years passed, and the war ended. Molly's kittens grew up to be bigger than their mother, but she had more, and you could tell the seasons by her litters. In the spring and again in the fall, she would disappear for days. The first time it happened, Rico was crushed.

But one day Molly would come home, her sides already beginning to swell, her calico spots sleek and shining, her eyes content. She always had four babies, and strangely, there was always one calico, two oranges, and a black. The black was always a runt.

The neighborhood filled up with cats. In time,

because they were often fierce hunters, the rat population died down. Mr. Frisbie took in one of Molly's runts and even called it Timothy because Rico named all the runts Timothy. My parents kept a calico. But to the day she died at thirteen, Molly had eyes for only one boy. She was always Rico's cat.